PETER BRADSHAW is the au   *Jesus* (1999), *Dr Sweet And His* *Triumph* (2013), and regularly writes for radio and television. His selected reviews in *The Films That Made Me* (2019) represent his work at *The Guardian,* where he has been chief film critic since 1999. He lives in London with his wife, the research scientist Dr Caroline Hill, and their son.

THE BODY IN THE MOBILE LIBRARY

& other stories

PETER BRADSHAW

Lightning Books

Published in 2024
by Lightning Books
Imprint of Eye Books Ltd
29A Barrow Street
Much Wenlock
Shropshire
TF13 6EN

www.lightning-books.com

ISBN: 9781785633904

Cover design by Nell Wood
Illustration by Heather Heyworth
Typeset in Dante and Impact Label Reversed

British Library Cataloguing in Publication Data

A catalogue record for this book is available from the British Library.

For Sarah and Roy

CONTENTS

THE KISS

To celebrate the election of Winston Churchill as Prime Minister in 1951, a former officer in the Polish air force called Tadeusz Andrzejewski bought a drink for a woman he'd only just met. This was in The Bell in Hendon, North West London. Elspeth Pierce was a seamstress at the Golders Green Hippodrome; she was a divorced woman in her early forties with a pretty smile. Tadeusz was still a virgin, despite having reached the age of twenty-five and seen dangerous action in the last war.

'Ooh, may I have a ciggie?' was how Elspeth had struck up the conversation.

'Of course – but how did you know I smoked?' Tadeusz had smilingly replied. He had not actually had a cigarette in his mouth, or any pack visible.

'I just guessed.'

They had lit up, and after some explanation of his accent, Tadeusz asked if she had been up all night for the election. Elspeth replied that it had been a while since she had been up all night. Tadeusz agreed, but said that he had actually stayed up late because he was pleased for Mr Churchill. He had asked what she might like to drink. Elspeth asked for a Gin and It; Tadeusz got himself another pint of bitter, and they carried on talking.

'So why are you not at work?' Elspeth asked.

'I'm a student,' Tadeusz replied. 'I'm studying philosophy at Queen Mary's College.'

'Are you indeed? And you're in here, philosophising!'

'Yes! Yes, I am.'

'And what's your philosophy, may I ask?'

Tadeusz, amazing himself with his forwardness, took Elspeth's hand.

'My philosophy is: seize the day.'

'Gosh, mine too.'

They finished their drinks and Tadeusz bought the same again.

'So what are you doing here in the afternoon, Elspeth?' he asked, once they were settled again and talking about her job.

'Well, there's not much for me to do,' she replied. 'There's no matinee today.'

She was working on a show called *For The Fun Of It*. They talked a little about that, and both silently noticed that the saloon was now entirely empty; they had a sort of privacy. Even the landlord was serving customers over in the public bar. This was not to say that another drinker might not come in at any moment.

'I think you should be on the stage,' said Tadeusz,

extravagantly. 'You're much prettier than all those girls!'

'Thank you darling!' Elspeth exclaimed brightly, then leaned forward and kissed him on the lips.

The kiss continued. Elspeth's tongue swarmed into Tadeusz's mouth, and he set his glass back down on the table with a bang: it nearly spilt. They carried on kissing, and Tadeusz placed his hand on Elspeth's right breast. She pushed his hand away but carried on with the kiss. Tadeusz now had a very painful erection. Finally, they broke apart and smiled shyly at each other. Hardly knowing what to do or say, Tadeusz fumblingly took out a ten-pound note and made to go up to the bar for more drinks, but Elspeth stopped him.

'Don't spend your money on drinks,' she whispered to him. 'Let's go back to my flat. Brent Street. Do you know it?'

Tadeusz nodded quickly and emphatically, like a child.

Elspeth leaned in closer. 'Do you have a French letter, Tadeusz?' she murmured.

'Back at my digs.'

'Go and fetch it, darling, and meet me at 97B, Brent Street.'

They both rose, Tadeusz a little unsteadily, and parted at the door; he hurried downhill to his rooms in Stratford Road and Elspeth more calmly went up towards her place.

Tadeusz did indeed have a contraceptive at his lodgings, and could hardly believe that he was now about to put it to use. He walked more quickly.

As for Elspeth, she had a way of asking her new gentlemen friends for presents and was adept at timing the question. As Tadeusz was undressing in her bedroom, she would say something like: 'Can I have that ten pounds, now, ducks?' implying that they had already discussed the matter. The poor boy would be too embarrassed to make a fuss, too ashamed to admit that he had misunderstood the situation, too mortified to confess he genuinely thought he was so attractive as to sweep a woman off her feet at five minutes' notice in the middle of the afternoon. He would hand over the money as meek as a lamb and they would go ahead. Elspeth could later, of course, with many forgiving endearments, tell Tadeusz she didn't do this for just anyone, and that he was special.

Now trembling almost uncontrollably, Tadeusz arrived at his own front door and let himself in with his latch-key. He couldn't help imagining Elspeth in her underclothes, and then in no clothes at all.

He kept his contraceptive hidden. It wasn't in his rooms, where he knew his landlady would discover it, but in a concealed ledge by the steps in the building's cellar, a gloomy, cavernous and frankly noisome space. It actually descended two levels below the ground, but the lower floor had been damaged by a bomb in the war. A brick staircase took you down eight steps and below that there was a void, a dark, empty and dusty vault. It was also very cold.

Tadeusz opened the door and pressed the light switch. Nothing. The bulb must have gone since he was last down here. He gingerly took two steps further and felt along the grimy brick levels to his right. Where was that contraceptive sheath? He couldn't see. Angry and impatient, Tadeusz felt for his matches and, while both of his hands were thrust deep into his pockets, he stumbled and fell fifteen feet, head-first onto the stone surface below. He broke his neck, lost consciousness and died.

Tadeusz had made no noise, and the cellar door had swung closed behind him. Nobody had noticed him come in. He lay there, in the utter darkness, his feet pointing towards the front of the house, facing up, having effectively performed a twin-phase somersault on hitting the ground. The hours until teatime went by. Other tenants gathered in the dining room above for the evening meal and many people remarked on Tadeusz's absence, particularly his landlady, Mrs Price. His rent, which he had paid three months in advance, was for half-board: bed, breakfast and evening meal, prepared in Mrs Price's notoriously reeking kitchen. In Brent Street, Elspeth assumed that he had got cold feet and equably prepared for the evening's work.

The days went by and Tadeusz's disappearance became a subject of general conversation. A college official called at the house to ask if anyone knew of any reason why Mr Andrzejewski was persistently absenting himself from lectures and tutorials. Mrs Price telephoned the police and wrote to Lt Cmdr Richard Wilson, the RAF officer who had provided her with a reference for Tadeusz. Both were unable to help; the assumption was that he had simply gone home. Both his parents were dead and there were no relatives to notice his absence. Eventually Mrs Price re-let his room after confiscating and selling its contents: clothes, books. There was also an envelope containing fifty pounds in cash, which she quietly took and did not mention in her many shrill complaints about the situation.

Tadeusz's rigor mortis relaxed. His face, quite invisibly in the cellar's darkness, became ashy white as the blood settled on the underside of his body, but his arms and legs, again quite invisibly, turned an inky blue-black. His skin progressively dried out and shrivelled and made his hair and nails stand out the more starkly. His eyes, initially closed, half-opened in the dark as the eyelids contracted.

His lower intestine began to decompose, as micro-organisms broke down the dead cells. A greenish-brown patch began to spread across Tadeusz's lower stomach, a sticky, damp mass of blisters, which stuck to and then ate through his vest and into his shirt, his trousers and his underpants. The putrefaction had begun. Bacteria spread through the body: the rotting advanced up his chest and down into his legs, and those two inert black flesh logs began to ooze and sweat decay. Presently, there was not a square inch of his clothing which was not saturated with degenerate matter. Internal gases pushed his intestines out through his rectum, and after two weeks, his stomach split along the fault line of a war wound with a report that was quite loud, but inaudible to anyone in the building.

The smell was not remarked upon by Mrs Price and her tenants, as the lower floors of her building were oppressed by the odours of her unclean kitchen, and the ventilation in the two icily cold basement levels was such that most of the odour was neutralised.

As the months went by, the decomposition continued in such a way that Tadeusz's body mass diminished very considerably. Within a year, it was reduced and flattened, and a year after that it was hardly more than a dark, waxy outline upon the floor; the sticky, matted clothes gave it what substance it had. His skull was propped up at the top: a black cratered orb. The jaw became detached and rolled off Tadeusz's right shoulder and onto the floor.

The years passed, the fifties became the sixties, and Tadeusz's skeleton continued to thin down in the unvisited gloom. His bones, though ashier and more attenuated, continued to be an intelligible form. Mrs Price died in 1964 and her son, who wished in any case to emigrate to Australia, had no interest in managing a rooming house. And then the property, like everything else in the street, was subject to a compulsory purchase order, because the whole terrace was to be demolished to make way for three fifteen-storey blocks of flats.

The wrecking ball went through the buildings with an almighty crash and they collapsed heavily. Tons of masonry descended on Tadeusz's remains and whatever unwitnessed form they had had for the previous fifteen years was, in a moment, utterly effaced. Some clearance was made and by the end of the decade the concrete foundations were being poured down into the vacant lot. The cement formed an undifferentiated mixture with the black atoms of Tadeusz's residue, and above, the buildings climbed – three stark towers whose lift shafts and stairwells were always haunted by the howling of winds. As the seventies were succeeded by the eighties, Tadeusz's molecules stayed constant in their cement animation, while the buildings became a notorious site for crime and drug dealing, but in the nineties the authorities discovered that this could be deterred simply by changing the open-plan design to make the premises secure. A front door would be added, with an entry code known only to vetted residents.

The twenty-first century dawned, with many of these flats sold off to their tenants or to other buyers: now they were desirable properties with excellent views over London and Middlesex. Their prices climbed, stalled a little with the crisis of 2008, and climbed again. But the dust got in from the pavement, and the sound of the wind was unceasing.

REUNION

In a quiet moment during a business trip, Elliot Chatwin reflected that he had been in love three times during his life. Once, while married and in his early forties, with Joan – a colleague. They were having an affair, although neither said that word out loud. Once before that, in his early thirties, with Michiko – who was now his ex-wife. And once when he was just eleven years old, with Lucy Venables, the girl who lived next door. She was also eleven.

Sitting on the bed in his hotel room, Elliot took a moment to consider the three affairs, and the three break-ups.

Easily the most painful was with Joan. He had scheduled one of their semi-regular dinner dates that often led to something back at her apartment. He had been a little bit early, sitting at a table, working up the courage to make some sort of declaration to her, trying to think what he might say, when Joan turned up and started saying, on sitting down, that she had fallen in love with somebody else, and they were moving in together. Elliot nodded his absolute and immediate acceptance of this situation. He even did a lip-biting little smile, taking it well, like a reality TV contestant getting told he's not going through to the next round. Joan had said that, under the circumstances, it was probably better if they postponed dinner until some other time, having not in fact taken her coat off. She had never looked more beautiful, more strong and free.

With Michiko, it was in fact some time after that, in Tokyo, where they had gone for her mother's funeral. After the ceremony, back at her family home, the couple had sat silently on a squashy black leather couch with disconcertingly ice-cold aluminium armrests. Michiko had asked quietly where he would be living when they returned to London. She looked stylish and slim: quite ten years younger.

And as for the last case? There had been no break-up as such, but his unrequited adoration for Lucy Venables had been just as real, just as painful, just as all-consuming as any of his other loves. He felt it was entirely correct to count it as one of the big affairs. In fact, he was inclined to think it was the grandest and most intense passion of the three.

Elliot smiled sadly to himself as he undressed in his hotel room, preparing to have a shower before attending that evening's corporate cocktail party. What on earth had made him think of Lucy Venables after all this time?

Heaven knows, it was a disagreeable subject. Lucy Venables never loved him; she was wayward and capricious, and his last glimpse of Lucy was of her cruel little smile, looking on as her father gave him a slap across the face. In his adult life, Elliot had psychologically suppressed the memory of this, almost in its entirety.

Lucy Venables. Lucy Venables. Why was he thinking about Lucy Venables?

Subliminal images of her face, her house and her back garden had flashed into his mind that afternoon, after he had gone back into his room having attended a presentation at which all the other conference delegates were present. Like them, Elliot was involved in the solar panel industry. He had seen a sea of faces there. Could it conceivably be that a familiar set of features had been among them?

Elliot dismissed the idea with a smile and a tiny, audible laugh – a theatrical display of self-reproach for his own benefit. He showered, changed and turned up at the drinks reception which was being held in the hotel's large and very dull function room, bordered on one side by a floor-to-ceiling glass wall with doors at either end. This looked out onto a landscaped garden which sloped down to an artificial lake. It was as manicured as a golf course. With every glance he took at this panorama, it had got darker, as night was falling and what he saw was the yellowish reflection of the room's interior. Then this grassy expanse was suddenly re-illuminated by the electric lights positioned along the path that ran outside alongside the glass partition.

There was desultory conversation, not much helped by the name-tags that everyone was asked to wear; his read 'Mr Chatwin'. Waiters circulated with drinks. The canapés were meagre. Elliot repeatedly allowed his glass to be refilled and as the evening wore on he felt quite drunk. He needed a cigarette. Smoking here was forbidden, of course. He wondered if he might smoke outside, on that large artificial lawn beyond the glass. This wasn't at all certain. The no-smoking rules in hotels and public spaces extended outside in many areas nowadays. Elliot was just resolving to walk through the lobby area and out into the front car park – where he would surely be allowed to smoke – when suddenly he noticed something.

There was a woman, out there on the grass in the semi-darkness, smoking, with her back to him. Elliot had a strange feeling. Almost without knowing what he was doing, he absented himself from the party, walked out through one of the doors and headed across the Astroturf straight for her, with a half-formed idea about asking for a light.

Twenty paces away, Elliot paused, veering away, losing his nerve. He pretended to look out at the almost dark horizon, gazing in the same direction as the woman – and he made some play with getting out his cigarettes and tapping one against the pack. He sneaked a sidelong glance at her: a very attractive woman of about his age, smoking contemplatively, her right elbow in her left hand.

Was it…? Could it actually be…? There was nothing else for it. He would have to approach her.

'Excuse me,' he said. 'I wonder if you….'

She turned to face him, and immediately gaped in dawning recognition. Her name tag read: 'Ms Venables'. She was positively open-mouthed at the sight of him – and seeing his 'Mr Chatwin' she clapped the hand that wasn't holding the cigarette over her mouth. Then she removed it and said: 'Elliot! Oh my God! Oh my God! Is it you? Elliot!'

'Hi, hello,' said Elliot, hardly knowing what else to say.

'Oh my God! Elliot! This is so weird! I was thinking about you this afternoon! Just now! So weird!'

'Yes, as a matter of fact, I was thinking ab—'

'Oh my God! So weird! I was thinking of that time in our

back garden! With the darts! And Dad hitting you! Oh my God! And we never got a chance to talk to you or say sorry or anything!'

She was clearly drunker than he was. Elliott smiled self-deprecatingly, and made a gesture, as if to wave all these considerations away.

'Do you remember me, Elliot?' she then asked.

'Of course,' he replied.

'And all that with my dad…and the darts… I'm so sorry! Gosh, do you know for years after that I used to think of you.'

'Oh, I really don't remember too much about it…' Elliot said airily, with a smile.

This was quite untrue. Elliot remembered everything about it, and the whole history now came back into his mind, in every detail, with immense clarity and force. Lucy Venables' family moved into the house next to his at the beginning of the baking summer of 1976. Elliot was an only child with few friends, and one endless hot day, he was riding his bicycle round and round on the flagstones of his front yard, where his dad's car would be when he was not at work. He was seeing how tiny he could make the circle without falling off, and listening to his transistor radio playing Elton John and Kiki Dee singing 'Don't Go Breaking My Heart'. The sharp orchestral stabs and the repeated vocals used to go round and round in Elliot's head:

Don't go breaking my

Don't go breaking my

Eventually, he toppled over – with a clumsy semi-dismount, jabbing his thigh on the saddle. He heard a giggle and turned to see Lucy staring at him.

'You're not very good at that, are you?' she said pertly.

Elliot would at any other time have hotly insisted that he was, but now felt compelled to agree with this pretty stranger.

'Why don't you come next door, for some lemonade?' she then asked, and Elliot said OK.

They went through Lucy's front door, through the hall and into the kitchen.

Lucy poured out two glasses of Corona lemonade from a bottle taken from the fridge and they went out into the garden. There they mutely looked at Lucy's swingball set for a moment, until Lucy's mother appeared, with Lucy's little sister.

'Hello!' she said brightly. 'You must be Elliot. I had a nice chat with your mum yesterday, Elliot. We have to go now. Lovely that you've made friends with Lucy. Bye!'

Lucy and Elliot played swingball for a bit; Elliot's reasonable skill in the game entirely deserted him and Lucy always won. They had some more lemonade and soon it was time for him to go.

Every day this scene would repeat itself. Without ever arranging it in advance, Elliot would hang around outside his house or on the pavement, and Lucy would come out and invite him in to play in her garden. They would play Robin Hood and Maid Marian, doctors and nurses, mummies and daddies. Silly baby stuff, considering that they were eleven-year-olds. But Lucy would always insist and Elliot could soon think of nothing else but pleasing her.

He fell in love with Lucy. There was just no other way to describe it. And it was made more poignant and intense for the lack of anything he could remotely recognise as sexual desire – merely a hot, sick feeling in his tummy. And when Lucy would start to make fun of him and be cross with him, as she always did, the feeling was even worse.

It all came to a head one Saturday afternoon, while Elliot was over at Lucy's. Both her parents and her little sister were somewhere in the house. Sometimes the sister would wander out into the garden, to be sharply dismissed with a 'Go away, Chloë!' It was hot and Elliot was listless, and would not respond to her teasing and taunting. What was the matter, Lucy had asked. Elliot wouldn't reply. She persisted, and finally he spoke up.

'May I give you a kiss?' he asked.

'What?' Lucy tried to sound derisive and mocking, but in truth she was taken aback.

'I said: may I give you a kiss?'

Lucy was silent. As she pondered her reply – and as Elliot stared down at the ground, blushingly astonished at his own boldness – little Chloë came sauntering shyly out into the garden. Suddenly, Lucy said to her: 'Come here!'

Obediently, she followed as Lucy led over to the garden shed, whose door had a dartboard and three darts. She plucked out the darts, opened out the door, stood Chloë up against it and, taking a box of coloured chalks from somewhere inside the shed, proceeded to draw a loose outline around the little girl's head and shoulders, about twelve inches clear. Then Lucy offered the darts to Elliot.

'There. If you can throw all three darts so they stick in the door, inside the line, but without hitting Chloë, then I'll kiss you.'

Saucer-eyed, Chloë stayed perfectly still against the shed door, clutching her little doll, evidently content to be permitted to join her sister's game on any basis.

'OK,' said Elliott numbly, taking the darts and positioning

himself about seven feet away. He sized up his first throw, the dart-point lined up at eye-level, rocking back and forth on the balls of his feet – and then threw.

THUNK!

The dart landed just above the crown of little Chloë's head.

'Well done,' said Lucy coolly. 'One down; two to go.'

Elliot cleared his throat. After a few more little feints, he threw the second dart.

THUNK!

This one landed just to the left of Chloë's neck, inside the line. It counted. But now the little girl's lower lip was trembling; her eyes brimmed and she was starting to shift alarmingly about.

'Stay still, Chloë!' ordered Lucy. 'All right, Elliot. Third and last dart. Get this right, and it'll be a very big kiss for you.'

Elliot's hand trembled. He seemed to lose his nerve just as he was sizing up the third throw. He exhaled heavily, the dart clenched in his fist down at his side. Then he raised it and prepared again. He threw. A clumsy one. The dart flew in the direction of Chloë's left eye. She flinched, turned; it jabbed into the side of her ear. Chloë put her hand up to it; a trickle of blood ran down her forearm and for a moment it looked as if the dart was actually embedded in the side of her head.

Poor, panicky Elliot ran up and pulled away the dart. He thought he could actually hear the flesh of the little girl's ear ripping. She screamed, and it was at this moment that Lucy's father came running out into the garden. Elliot's little victim ran up to him and hugged him around the waist, sobbing desperately. Her blood was getting on his trousers.

'What the bloody hell's going on here?' he thundered.

'Elliot was playing a sort of William Tell game daddy,' said

Lucy with a sweet smirk.

Her father coldly walked up to Elliot and smacked him once across the face – and then stood aside as Elliot blubberingly ran out through the kitchen and back to his house. Quite soon after that, Lucy's family moved away and he never saw them again.

That is all that he could remember.

He was sure as he could be that this was what had happened. The woman now in front of him gave him a very familiar-looking smirk. That summer came rushing back, and with it the maddeningly catchy pop refrain in his head.

Don't go breaking my

Don't go breaking my

Elliot felt uncomfortable. He felt strangely intimate with this quasi-stranger, with whom the only thing he had in common was a bizarre episode decades before. And yet something in the situation's unreality was liberating, even exciting.

'Daddy used to talk about you a lot over supper,' she said. 'I think he knew he shouldn't have hit you.'

'Oh, I really can't remember,' he replied.

They were standing flirtatiously close.

'I don't think you ever got that kiss, did you?' she said.

'No,' said Elliot, nullifying the effect of his previous claim. 'Well, I wasn't entitled to it.'

'This party is very boring,' she said.

'Yes.'

'Why don't you come up to my room and I'll give you a kiss now.'

She turned on her heel and went back through the now thinning party and into the foyer. Elliot followed.

They got into the lift, in which they were alone. They kissed.

Once at the sixth floor, they got out and headed for her room three doors along. Once inside, they kissed again, rolling on the big double-bed. Elliot began clawing her clothes off and, panting, she plucked at his belt.

'Oh Elliot!' the woman gasped. 'Call me by my name. Say my name.'

She swept up her hair to reveal her cut and disfigured ear. 'Call me Chloë.'

THE BODY IN THE MOBILE LIBRARY

By the time DI Alex Greer and DI Jeff Wetherfield arrived at the crime scene, it was already taped off and the road closed. Uniforms crawling all over it. DI Wetherfield threw the half-filled Styrofoam cup of coffee he had with him into a bin; DI Greer dropped a lit cigarette on the pavement and twisted it out with his toe.

The scene itself, enclosed within the fluttering yellow ribbon, was actually a parked vehicle, the size of a lorry or two camper vans. Neither man knew quite what to make of it. The coachwork was a deep burgundy or brownish purple, with a kind of running board that swooped or curved at the rear of the vehicle into the entrance point, like a London Routemaster bus. It looked as if it had been designed some time during the Second World War.

DI Greer ducked under the tape which Wetherfield plucked

up with his finger and thumb, and DI Wetherfield himself followed.

'What is this thing?' asked DI Greer of a white-clad forensic officer, carrying a clipboard, on his way out.

'It's a mobile library,' said the man. 'Buses full of books. Hertfordshire County Council sends them out to places where normal library facilities are inaccessible. It's been coming here to Bricket Wood every other Thursday since 1974. Quite a dinosaur in the age of the internet. Ha!' The officer gestured vaguely. 'It usually parks up near the little parade of shops. But this morning they found it here. In the street.'

With a curt and uncomprehending nod, DI Greer dismissed the officer who walked off to his car, and the two men climbed into the library. They really did have to climb: the two steps were steep, and each had dozens of metal ridges, like an escalator. Inside was a corridor-type space, wide enough for two adults to pass each other with difficulty, in which one could walk up and down the length of the vehicle looking around at the high surrounding shelves crammed with books, although there were also CDs and old-fashioned videocassette boxes. A glass panel at the opposite end showed that the driver's seat was empty, and it also cast weak daylight on the scene which now presented itself to the two officers.

The body of a middle-aged man, wearing a suit jacket and waistcoat, but no trousers or underpants, appeared slumped at the level of their feet, as if he had been sitting on the floor with his back against the wall of books, and then slid downwards. Around his bulging throat was a heavy belt buckled into a noose, the far end of which was attached through the farthest hole to some kind of hook or clip above his head near the shelf marked Historical Fiction. His eyes were open and staring, and his tongue was lolling out of his mouth. In his left hand was an empty half-bottle of white rum. His large penis was fully erect, apparently in a state between priapism and rigor mortis, and a slug-trace of dried semen was visible on the lower part of the waistcoat.

'Oh my God,' said DI Greer.

'Yeah. Right,' said DI Wetherfield.

'No, I mean this guy. He's Dickon, my sobriety buddy.'

DI Greer had met Dickon Pachsman eighteen months previously, at his first AA meeting in St Albans. These sessions were held in the 'community space' adjoining the modern Presbyterian church. A trestle table bearing a hot-water urn, carton of milk and jar of instant coffee was set up at one end of the room, with half a dozen encrusted plastic spoons, and there was also a single dinner plate of chocolate digestive biscuits fanned out in a semi-circular presentation display. These went like lightning.

Those present sat on chairs arranged in a circle, rather than in rows facing the front, but Dickon was evidently first among equals as the convener of the group. He was dressed in cream slacks, and a V-necked navy-blue sweater over a salmon-pink shirt. Yet over this, in the American style, he had pulled a white T-shirt, bearing the legend: 'It Works If You Work It'. Towards the end of the evening, everyone saw on the back of the T-shirt: 'Keep Coming Back'.

'Hello everyone,' said Dickon in a gentle, calm voice. 'I'm Dickon.'

Everyone said: 'Hello Dickon,' and DI Greer wasn't sure if he should have joined in.

'I'd like to ask our newer members to introduce themselves first,' said Dickon. 'Lynn?'

Lynn was the only woman at the meeting, an extremely striking and composed-looking person with short dark hair and a waist-length leather jacket.

'Hello, I'm Lynn, and I'm an alcoholic.'

'Hello Lynn.'

'I drink because I need affirmation,' said Lynn calmly. 'I drink because I need love. For me, it got so that drink was love. What I want to say is that the social display of drinking is a male construct. For me, it got so that I would get drunk with men, married men, and I would have sex with them – five, six, seven times and then I would disappear from their lives, never contacting them ever again. I needed drink to do this: three, sometimes four glasses of wine.'

The men present received this testimony in thoughtful silence, nodding. The rate of the nodding accelerated as they realised she had finished.

'Lynn, thank you for sharing,' said Dickon, and paused.

'Thank you, Lynn,' everyone else said.

'Now, Alex, perhaps you could tell us something about yourself,' said Dickon, turning his gentle smile on Greer.

DI Greer felt a twinge of stage fright, nastier than anything he had experienced in the line of duty.

'Yes,' he said, redundantly. 'My name is, my name is Alex Gr—.' He realised that he was about to give his full name and rank, as if giving evidence in court.

But the group interrupted, insistently, all with the same encouraging smile. 'Hello, Alex,' they said.

'I'm here because I drink a lot.'

He caught Dickon's eye. The group's convenor regarded him with mild reproof at this obvious evasion.

'I'm here because I drink too much.' Alex went on,

correcting himself, but of course quite well aware that even this formulation fell short of what was expected. 'It was beginning to affect my work.'

DI Greer fell silent and Dickon prompted: 'Go on, Alex.'

'The worst moment came when a colleague and I had to interrogate a suspect. We'd had him in custody since six and I came on duty around half-past. I'd been drinking all day.'

Everyone in the group leaned forward slightly. Even Dickon seemed to appreciate the suspense.

'The guy had been arrested on suspicion of... Well, I don't want to go into the details. It was to do with kids.'

There was pin-drop silence in the room.

'My colleague Jeff had been questioning him in the absence of his brief. You're not supposed to do that. But he hadn't turned the tape on and the interview room video wasn't working. We'd seen to that. As I approached the room, Jeff went out to take a call and left me to it. I knew I was drunk. I'd totally fucking lost it. On my way there, I grabbed a biro off one of the tables, popped the cap off and held it like this, like a dagger.'

DI Greer demonstrated the downward-blade grip in his empty fist. The lips of every person in the room were slightly parted.

'I got nearer and nearer the interview room. I knew he was in there. A fucking red mist went down. And then, when I was a couple of yards from the door, I turned and saw the computer terminal on someone's desk was on YouTube and he was watching this video of a kitten pulling on a balaclava and I just started laughing so much, it was so cute, I just had to sit down. I was laughing hysterically. It was later agreed I should get some therapy for my mood swings. And obviously my drinking.'

There was a pause.

'OK, well, thank you Jeff,' said Dickon, and there was a murmured repetition of the words. 'Thank you for sharing. That was very courageous of you. We always say in this group: emotional concealment is emotional congealment.'

After the session was over, Dickon approached DI Greer privately.

'Alex, I liked what you had to say just now.'

'Mm, right,' said DI Greer, impatient to be off.

'Alex, don't be scared to ask for help.'

'No. I mean I'm not.'

'Alex, I want to be your sobriety buddy.'

'What?'

'Your sobriety buddy, Alex. I prefer it to the more conventional "sponsor". I can help you put your sobriety at the centre of your life. But also friendship. A friend who knows what you are going through. It's as much about the buddy as it is about the sobriety.'

'Right.'

'What's your mobile? I can text you my number.'

He did so, and DI Greer left.

Five weeks after that, a period in which his abstinence from alcohol had felt increasingly like having an operation without anaesthetic, DI Greer was desperate for a drink. It had been a hard day. He dreamed about a glass of Merlot. He fantasised about a pitcher of ice-cold lager. At seven in the evening, DI Greer was on his knees in the kitchen, staring with fanatical concentration into the fridge at a bottle of Muscadet, scrutinising the tiny droplets on the surface of the glass. He had already eaten, so it wasn't as though it would be on an empty stomach. He badly needed someone to talk him down.

He remembered Dickon, his sobriety buddy.

DI Greer kept it together: he stood up, went into the living room, found the mobile in his jacket and called Dickon.

The number rang five times, then went to voicemail. DI Greer just hung up and in a mood of angry despair headed back in the direction of the fridge, with every intention of opening the bottle. But then his phone rang.

'Alex? Alex mate. Is that you? Was… Were you ringing me? Oh shit.'

DI Greer could hear something falling onto the floor and breaking.

'Yes, Dickon. Look, I'm in a bit of trouble. I need to talk. I admit it. I need to talk. I think I'm coming off the wagon.'

'What? Jesus. I'll drive round to yours right away.'

'You sound strange. Sort of snuffly.'

'Yeah, I've got a cold. Plus, I'm arseholed.'

Before DI Greer could reply, the line went dead and Dickon arrived ten minutes later; Greer could hear his car hitting the wheelie recycling bins outside the front entrance to his building. He buzzed Dickon up, opened the flat door and his guest blundered in, and leant unsteadily against the wall, breathing through his mouth.

Then he slumped onto the couch. Both men said nothing.

'I think I'd better have some coffee,' said Dickon sheepishly.

With a full cafetière in front of him, a small jug of milk and two cups, Dickon opened up.

'I never meant for this to happen. You can imagine how I feel. I had five hundred days, Alex. Five hundred days of sobriety. And now this. Sorry about your bins, incidentally.'

For his part, DI Greer found he had no more desire for a

drink. He asked: 'What happened?'

'It's all your fault, Alex.'

'What?'

'Well, not exactly. It all started to go wrong once I agreed to be your sobriety buddy.'

'Agreed? You were the one who—'

'Before that, I was also Lynn's sobriety buddy. Actually, a bit more than that. I turned into her sobriety lover. And then her sobriety fiancé. I had to tell her that my sobriety monogamy was going to have to be transferred temporarily to you. Sort of sobriety man-ogamy. Ha! Things haven't been easy.'

'Can't you be sobriety-whatever to more than one person?'

'That's hardly the point, Alex. It was what you shared in the group. All that stuff about police work. It hurt me.'

Dickon poured some milk into his coffee, spilling it onto the table, and took a long slurp.

'You see, before I lost my job I was an academic criminologist. I wrote my thesis on the police officer in pop culture and the media. It was great. I would lecture all over the country. Seminars. Webinars. My contribution to the Festschrift for our outgoing head of department more or less tore up the rule book. So when some cash went missing one day from the Criminology budget, I was the obvious person to head up the internal investigation. I was drinking pretty heavily and my interrogation methods were, unfortunately, influenced by a research paper I had just written about cultural representations of the Birmingham Six. I was sacked. Now the only work I can get is driving this stupid mobile library van around the place. And I'll lose that if I lose my licence.'

There was silence. Both men listened to the traffic outside. Dickon smiled weakly.

'It seems like I'm giving you my testimony, now,' he said.

'Dickon,' said DI Greer, standing up and looking out of the window. 'Do you think anyone is ever truly free of their addictions?'

He turned around, expecting an answer, but Dickon was now asleep, his head slumped forward, mouth slack but upright seated posture unaltered, and Greer had to rescue the tilting mug from his fist.

DI Weatherfield listened to DI Greer telling him all this, and his eyes never left Dickon's bloated, distended corpse, slumped at one end of the mobile library. When Greer stopped speaking, Weatherfield looked at him with infinite patience and calm.

'I remember that YouTube video,' he said, quietly. 'It was hilarious.'

'So I guess it's an open-and-shut case of suicide, then?'

'Not necessarily,' said Weatherfield, reaching into Dickon's jacket pockets, feeling around, and finally extracting a mobile phone, whose 'contacts' list he located, and began to search under the letter L.

'Are you Lynn Edwards?' asked Weatherfield, as a woman with short dark hair and a waist-length leather jacket answered the door.

'Yes.'

'Then perhaps we could ask you a few questions,' he said, barging in, snatching the Evian bottle from her hand, sniffing the clear liquid inside, grimacing, and passing it to Greer who sniffed, grimaced and found he had nowhere to put it.

Lynn stood in the hall, looking stricken.

'We are investigating the death of Mr Dickon Pachsman,

who I understand was your sobriety buddy.'

Wetherfield took a step towards Lynn and fixed her with a challenging glare. 'Is there anything you wish to tell us?'

It was a bold gamble and it paid off.

'I admit it,' sobbed Lynn, her chin bobbing down on her chest. 'I did it. Getting Dickon to go too far with auto-erotic strangling games in his mobile library wasn't too difficult. Neither was making it look like suicide.'

'He was your sobriety buddy?' asked Greer.

Lynn turned to DI Greer, her eyes flashing with anger.

'He was my ex-sobriety buddy.'

That afternoon, DI Greer gazed out over the allotments and chimneypots from the panorama window in his eighth-floor apartment in Watford. It gave him a fine view of the hospital and the football ground. There were stories like Dickon's all over Hertfordshire, he reflected: unquiet souls were going in and out of their homes and workplaces like honeybees in a hive, working, working, working, worrying, worrying, worrying. And for what?

In the skies above him darkness was arriving, and with it an awful sense of foreboding.

SENIOR MOMENT

Ivor Frederick Jones was in the basement-level men's room of a handsomely converted country-house hotel when he found that he could not remember his middle name. He had just finished urinating, and was examining a framed hunting print hanging in front of his face, showing the surrounding countryside. A Boxing Day Meet: 1910. How many years ago was that, he wondered?

It was on trying to calculate the sum in his head that he made the discovery that his middle name had mysteriously vanished. There was a mental gap, or dip, between his first and last names. A caesura. His middle name's disappearance upended all efforts to subtract 1,910 from the current year, and when he cautiously attempted to establish some known quantities by remembering his first name, and came up at first merely with Iran and Iraq, he stood there, still as a post, the thumb and forefinger of his right hand resting lightly on the top of his emptied penis, and those of this other massaging the skin above the bridge of his nose.

Another man came in to use the urinal next to him. Hurriedly, to avoid the appearance of impropriety, he finished up, hunching out his coccyx and, bending his knees slightly, squatting his pelvis down to squeeze out the last remaining drops of urine. When had he learned to do that? He zipped himself up and went over to the basin to wash his hands, all with the air of a man who was quite well aware what his middle and first names were, and noticed that the man was smiling at him in a friendly way, as if they knew each other. Ancient warnings about other men in public lavatories swam up into his mind. As the cold water ran, he wondered if he should take his wedding ring off to wash his hands – or if this might send a catastrophic message to the strange man. With a tiny start, he wondered if taking off his wedding ring before washing his hands was in any case something he habitually did.

iPad. Island. Icon. Eyelash. Ivor.

Ivor pulled his wedding ring up to the knuckle, where it was immobilised by a fat coronet of flesh; he repeated the manoeuvre twice and then returned the ring to its resting place. Ah. So he did not normally take his ring off. Ivor let the water run gently over his hands, remembering to slant them down so that his sleeves did not get wet, and considered whether and when to look up at his own reflection in the wide mirror that ran the length of the washbasins. The stranger joined him at the basin to his right.

'Lovely day,' the man said, and instantly Ivor knew that the innocuous observation was invested with more importance than usual, but still preoccupied with the loss of his middle name, could not quite see why. He smiled and nodded quickly to close down the conversation.

'Yes, lovely.'

'It really is smashing,' persisted the man, who then brought both sets of fingers and thumbs together and, like an orchestra conductor emphasising an important final chord, jabbed the two bird-beak forms of his hands at Ivor's lapels. 'You have organised the weather *beaut*-ifully! Ta-ra for now!'

He went. Ivor looked back at his face in the glass and was reassured by what he saw. The men's room had bathed it in an undersea greeny-blue light which smoothed away imperfections. His thick dark-grey hair, jowly face and unfashionable glasses all looked robust, strong, dependable. And fiercely alert.

Still worrying at this lapse of memory, Ivor wondered if now was the moment to leave the lavatory and – he forced himself to punctuate the silence with a little, exasperated laugh. Actually, what was he supposed to be doing? Who was he? Should he stay there for a little bit, to think about it?

His middle name would come to him in just a moment. It was, as you might say, on the tip of his tongue. It was stuck between two of his lower teeth. Ivor froze, allowing cold water to run over his hands. If he stayed perfectly still and kept calm, no one would notice anything was wrong. This tiny cloud would pass and he would not have embarrassed himself.

The urinals began to flush and rinse themselves. Ivor had now spent long enough in their presence to recognise the timer pattern on which they did so. Another man came in and, without responding to Ivor's thin, non-committal smile, went into one of the stalls. Ivor had a strong sense that it was time to leave.

The lavatory's exit led back out to a dark corridor, lined with hunting prints of a similar sort to the one he had been looking at. At one end were two doors that led respectively to the ladies' lavatory and to an office which was evidently off-limits. The wallpaper was vividly striped with pink and green, the colours of old-fashioned sweets. There were yet more hunting prints. Spindly horses and riders in full gallop. Also: a photocopying machine and some coat hooks. A young woman in a dark grey suit came out of the office door and told him what a lovely day it was. Ivor agreed.

When she had gone, he took a sheet of paper from the top of a pile by the photocopier and affected to be studying it, one hand stroking his upper lip, as he walked down the corridor towards what appeared to be the lobby. That way, if someone wondered what he was doing – well, he was detained by important business, reading this piece of paper about towels.

Ivor stopped by some sort of reception area, breezily delivered the document to the young woman on duty and, cheerfully assenting to her proposition that it hadn't been this nice all week, strode outside for a bit of a walk.

It began with F. Or perhaps it began with something that looked like F, like E, or sounded like F, like S. What was he doing here? It would come back to him in a minute. Something would bring it back to him. Gravel yielded under his footsteps with more of a pebbly rattle than a crunch, like an English beach holiday, the sort he was used to taking with his wife, whose name he remembered was Jill, a memory he elicited like bursting a blackhead. The branches of some plane trees framed a distant lake, which Ivor approached, and speculatively threw in one of the little stones. He even tried to make it skip, a knack that, he now remembered, had eluded him from his earliest boyhood.

Everyone had been right. It really was a glorious day. Perhaps he could stay here for a little while, perhaps stretch out on one of these armless benches and even sunbathe. Perhaps his middle name would just come back to him. Actually, Ivor had almost forgotten that he had forgotten. But the question of what exactly he was supposed to be doing just at that very minute came back with a cold and jarring blankness.

Perhaps he could pretend to have been mugged. That was it. He could find a heavy stone and hit himself over the head with it, and stagger around with his forehead trickling with blood. Asking for help would not therefore be a mortifying and humiliating experience. He had been mugged. He had lost his memory. Someone had hit him with this large rock and taken his wallet. He would of course have to throw his wallet away, to make the story look good. Or he would have to hide it. Hide it behind one of these bushes.

But wait. His wallet would have documentation in it, wouldn't it? Driving licence. Library card. Credit card. Something that might have his middle name. Something that would bring everything back to him. He might not have to smash himself over the head with a rock after all!

Ivor felt in his jacket pockets, but no wallet. Another thought struck him. Perhaps he had really been mugged. Perhaps someone had crept up behind him in that lavatory and assaulted him using a sinister martial arts technique, some deft, occult little jab to the skull which would result in no pain or bruising but would immobilise him for the fraction of a second needed to reach into his jacket and take the wallet. The sun came back out from behind a cloud and Ivor was momentarily blinded by the reflection from the water's surface. Someone spoke.

'Ivor. Ivor, hello.'

He turned and saw a well-dressed man, younger than he, whose head was inclined a little on one side, a man whose manner had been clearly modified in order to remove any obvious suggestions of urgency or alarm.

'Ivor, are you feeling all right?'

'I'm fine,' he replied smiling calmly. The question had told him that this was not the person to ask what his middle name was, or what on earth he was doing there. What was he doing there? Losing his middle name was like accidentally pulling out the plug with his toe, and now the bathwater of identity was draining away.

The man smiled too, and raised both palms while bending fractionally at the knees in a dumb show of appeasement.

'I'll leave you be for a bit.'

He disappeared, and Ivor went back to squinting at the lake. The man might have been a doctor, or a nurse, an official of some kind: he seemed to expect something of Ivor, and Ivor felt himself on the brink of realising what it was. If he could only find his wallet.

For the first time, he felt in his jacket pockets down by his hips and in one he felt a piece of paper, folded into four. He probed it with his fingertips, and felt the impress of handwriting in biro pushed through the paper like braille. His own handwriting. This was it. This was the document that would explain everything. And yet Ivor could not bring himself to snatch the piece of paper out of his pocket, unfold it and read – surely he should now be able simply to remember what it was and what it said? From resentment, from fear, he left it where it was.

Turning around, Ivor could now see a number of people spilling out onto the terrace at the back of the building, evidently looking at the lake as well. Among them, he could see a woman in a white dress. It looked exactly like Jill. But surely Jill was dead? The clothes gave her a sacrificial look, and Ivor's state of mind was complicated and made yet more disagreeable by a memory of the last argument he had had with Jill, an argument about a house not so different from this one. Ivor remembered dully how angry he had been with her.

But did this mean that he himself was dead, and everyone he had been talking to was dead? Ivor felt the sharp edges of the folded paper and suppressed the nausea and panic that were beginning to climb in his chest.

A second man appeared, an older man with a faint, interesting resemblance to the face he had seen in the lavatory mirror.

'Hello Ivor,' he said, and then, with a nervous laugh: 'Touch of nerves, is it?'

Ivor gave an ambiguous little smile and a 'hah!'.

'Well, we're all waiting for you.'

Ivor went back with the man. They even linked arms, like Edwardian swells, and were now intimate enough for Ivor to realise that the suit sleeves of his companion were worn and threadbare. As they made their way across the grass, back up to the terrace, the group of people, including the woman in white, murmured and smiled and even broke out into a little scatter of applause. Ivor felt a growing rush of confidence. Any second now it would come to back to him. He touched the folded paper.

His reappearance was evidently the signal for the entire

company to troop off the terrace, and process in front of him through an open set of French windows and into a large and well-appointed dining room, which was set for luncheon. Yes of course. Now he was so close to her, Ivor was sure the woman was his late wife, Jill, looking miraculously well and supernaturally young, though her cheeks sparkled with tears. It was like a dream. Perhaps she was crying about their last argument: the thought caused a tremor of resentment within him and he had half a mind to have it out with her, then and there. Yet all these people were taking their seats and the focus of attention was still on him. It was like a board or examination of some sort. Now Ivor still felt a growing, almost euphoric sense that his memory was imminently to be returned to him. He remained standing while everyone else sat down, and again noticed the threadbare feel of the man's suit sleeve.

His friend addressed the company in a loud voice: 'Ladies and gentlemen – the father of the bride!'

Ivor removed the piece of paper from his jacket pocket and unfolded it, now quite relaxed, but did not start to speak immediately.

Threadbare. Thread. Frederick. Frederick!

THE BINGO WINGS
OF THE DOVE

Jennifer knew that it was a wicked world. Charities employed telephone cold-callers to harass elderly people, cyclists mounted the pavement and gentle people with a lovely sense of humour were bullied off social media. It happened every day.

Jennifer knew the score. You needed to be a survivor. So when her older-by-ten-years boyfriend Malcolm suggested robbing the bingo stall at the local junior school's summer fête, Jennifer was so excited she initiated urgent love-making in the kitchen. It was a sensually abrasive congress of such abandon that Malcolm accidentally broke a tree of mugs with the back of his head.

'How much are they charging for each bingo card?' asked Jennifer later.

'One pound, or actually it could be one fifty.'

'And how many paying customers are we talking about?'

'Forty, or sixty; conceivably a hundred. Anyway, it's a lot. And the prizes are donated bottles of Pernod. So it doesn't come out of the ticket money. Really big score. Pure candy.'

'Nice one.'

Jennifer and Malcolm smoked weed for the rest of the afternoon to help them relax – and focus on the practicalities.

Malcolm actually knew about the bingo because Taylor, his son by a previous partner, had in fact been a pupil at Cobden Hill School, having left a few years before. This was before Malcolm's new relationship had begun. There was a regular summer fête. Local estate agents provided sponsorship and advertised the event with boards. Malcolm had helped with the tombola. But the real hit was the bingo, set up on the main playground by the entrance, under a tarp canopy in case the weather was bad. Malcolm had seen for himself the kind of money it brought in. People bought card after card. The money was kept in a cash box and when that was full, it was taken to a classroom where it was counted and bagged by two teachers and a parent, the sum recorded in a ledger, and then taken to the deputy headteacher's flat around the corner and finally deposited at the local branch of HSBC on Monday morning. The receipt was officially acknowledged at the next Parent Staff Association meeting.

Hundreds and hundreds of pounds.

Jennifer and Malcolm pondered this in silence in her bedroom. It could provide the cash float Jennifer needed to retrain as a doulah.

'It's a lot of money,' said Malcolm. 'But if you compare it to someone's money who's really rich, it's not.'

'No, I suppose not.'

This consideration in no way diminished his enthusiasm for the plan.

The day of the fête, which was the day of the heist, was muggy and warm.

Proceedings were opened by a former British middleweight boxing champion, now an elderly but good-natured figure, baffled when a very high-spirited Malcolm insisted on shadow-sparring with him as he walked up onto the wooden podium in the middle of the playground to address the crowd through a microphone.

When the boxer was finished, and was duly applauded, Malcolm then loudly announced to anyone who would listen that, sadly, he had to go and couldn't stay for the rest of the fête as he had an appointment somewhere. This was to establish his 'alibi', a part of the plan he had extensively discussed with Jennifer the previous evening, while drinking a six-pack of strong lager. He had not actually quite got round to finding anyone who might pretend to have been with him at the time of the crime, or to considering why he needed to have come to the fête in the first place. But there would be time enough later on. And if all went well, there would in any case be no need for any of this.

He walked briskly out of the playground, nodding curtly to the two teachers at the trestle table who had taken his 50p entry fee. Keyed up with excitement, he broke into a little jog as he made his way back to the flat. Once there he texted Jennifer: *will wait an hr then go back to the school wearing my balaclava*

Jennifer disconcertingly texted back: *y?*

He replied: *to hide my face*

She texted again: *y?*

And he replied: *cos today is the fuckin fate*

Malcolm angrily walked back and forth in his kitchen, ignoring Jennifer's final, penitent text: *oh yeah sorry*

Jennifer was on a train to see her mum in Berkhamsted. She had got it into her head the fête was the following Saturday, and probably would have cancelled or rearranged this trip if she had realised.

It was not a good omen.

Malcolm beguiled the time by smoking more strong weed. When he arrived back at the school, he realised he had actually forgotten to bring the balaclava, so resolved to conceal his identity by pulling his LA Lakers baseball cap down low over his face. This plan was undermined when the two teachers asked him for another 50p entrance fee as he stalked in, and he pulled up the cap, actually pointing to his face, and brusquely reminded them that he had already paid.

On the far north-east corner of the playground, he could see it: the bingo stall, under the tarp which actually provided some shade on this hot sunny day. There was a crowd there, and the headteacher, Mrs Frances Dellarussa, was doing the announcing, with jokey references to 'two fat ladies' and 'clickety-click'. There was also a young man with receding hair helping out. But the bingo did now seem to be on the verge of wrapping up. Malcolm knew that soon they would be folding up the bingo banner and collecting all the cards and then taking all of this, together with the cash, away to be counted. He should follow at a discreet distance.

But first he needed to go to the toilet.

When he came back from using the lavatories reserved for staff, Malcolm saw that the bingo stall had been swiftly and completely dismantled, including the tarp canopy. Not a sign of it was left. Some Year Six pupils with electric guitars were setting up for their Battle of the Bands. For the first time, Malcolm panicked. Where were the bingo people? Where on earth was the cash-box full of money that he was going to steal?

'Excuse me,' he said to two passing mums with babies in pushchairs. The second syllable had an aggressive nasal hoot which made these women step back in alarm, and the phrasing of what he said made them even more anxious.

'Where are the bingo people?'

As it happened, one of these women knew the answer. Mrs Dellarussa and the teaching assistant were in the headteacher's office, which he could reach via the classroom where they were standing, and then down the corridor. Malcolm took his leave of the two women without thanking them or saying goodbye.

When he blundered into the office, Mrs Dellarussa and her associate were looking at a glossy wallchart, taken from a Sunday newspaper, showing national dress for all the countries of the world. Malcolm took a breadknife from his jacket-pocket and brandished it at them.

'Gimme the money. Gimme the fuckin' money. Gimme the bingo money.'

There was a stunned silence, and finally Mrs Dellarussa spoke, her voice quavering.

'There is no money.'

'What?'

'People playing bingo don't give us any cash; they transfer money to our PayPal account with their smartphones.'

'Whaat?'

At this point, the young man with receding hair stepped in and repeated what Mrs Dellarussa had just told him: there was no cash. Everything was managed wirelessly. Malcolm continued to point the bread knife at them, angrily sceptical. 'Fuck off,' he said at last.

Then the young man looked closer at Malcolm, who had briefly pushed back his Lakers cap.

'Dad?' he said.

There was another long silence and now Malcolm said quietly: 'You. What?'

'Dad, it's me, Taylor.'

'Taylor?'

'Yes, Dad, please put that down. Are you all right? Have you been drinking?'

Malcolm sat down on one of the small classroom chairs. He did not put the knife away but continued to hold it, gazing at it, as if trying to guess how much it weighed.

'Taylor, how old are you? When did you leave here?'

'Ten years ago, Dad. Ten years ago.' Taylor felt emboldened to put some reproach into his voice. 'When you left Mum.'

'When…'

'I'm twenty-one, Dad. Thanks for the card. Thanks for the presents. I've got a job here now.'

'Twenty-one.'

'Yes.'

'Time just—'

Malcolm lost his precarious balance on the tiny classroom chair and slightly nicked the palm of his right hand with the knife. He stood up and his face went puce; he bit his trembling lip and shoved his right hand into his left armpit. There was an excruciating few seconds while he tried not to burst into tears.

Then he sobbed with his hands over his face; Taylor touched his arm and when Malcolm put his hands down, there was a small crescent of blood on his right cheek.

'I'm sorry,' he said. 'I'm sorry.'

Taylor and Mrs Dellarussa quietly conferred and the headteacher agreed to her employee's suggestion that, on this occasion, it would not be necessary to call the police.

In Malcolm's flat, Taylor put the kettle on and tried to find mugs. There weren't any, so he made tea in a dainty pair of unmatched, un-saucered cups, sharing a teabag. The daylight came in through the window in such a way as to pick out dust motes in the air and crumbs on the floor.

'How are you? How are you doing?'

Malcolm shrugged, smiled, reached for his Rizlas inside his jacket; at a sharp look from Taylor he placed his hands back on the kitchen table.

'I'm all right.'

'You don't look all right. Sorry not to see you at my twenty-first, Dad. You were invited.'

In answer, Malcolm made another sad shrug.

'What, you were busy?'

'I had stuff on.'

'So I see. How old are you, actually?'

'Forty-five. Halfway there.'

'Sorry?'

'Bingo lingo. Forty-five. Halfway there. There's ninety numbers. I'm forty-five. More than halfway there in my case.'

'Mm.'

'Are you still with that Russell?'

'Ronald. And yes I am. Are you with anyone at the moment?'

Malcolm's mobile phone made an audible buzz from inside his pocket. A text. He thought about the question and said: 'Not, no, no one serious, no.'

'Right.'

'Listen, I'm going to give up all this stuff and go back to meetings. I really am. I promise. I'm really sorry about today. It was a wake-up call.' Malcolm accompanied the phrase with a pious nod. 'Do you think you're going to get into trouble?'

'I'm not sure.'

'Key of the door,' said Malcolm smiling dreamily, because the phrase rhymed, and because of Taylor's age. 'Bingo. Two. Me and you. Two. Me and you.' He had his mobile phone out, looking happily at a message.

He closed his eyes. Taylor washed up the cups and let himself out.

HALF-CONSCIOUS
OF THE JOY

My name is Julian Smattering.

Before we begin, let me put you in the picture about my doctoral research. My thesis is entitled 'The Male Gaze In William Wordsworth'. There. I said it. You heard me. Male gaze. Boom! Is my research a rehearsal of liberal-humanist pieties about the organic flowering of literary genius? No. Is it a rigorous analysis of the way in which Wordsworth's poetry and its attendant critical response have been ideologically constructed? Yes. I'm all about the ideology.

This is the second year of my PhD on Wordsworth. I'm not just a primary scholarship person, a bits-of-paper person. I'm also an ideas person. I live in Archway in North London with my older-woman girlfriend Janine who works at Pret A Manger.

She's sort of the breadwinner.

As it happens, I do a fair bit of graft in the British Library in St Pancras: reading around the topic; secondary work; establishing the conceptual framework – that sort of thing. About a year ago I found myself outside the building having a cigarette and reading, again, something up on the wall, a cutesy bit of corporate whimsy sanctioned by the library authorities. 'You can never get a cup of tea large enough or a book long enough to suit me' – CS Lewis. Christ, that's irritating. Of course you can have cups of tea too big or books too long. Most books are too long. I can just see CS Lewis and his great ugly face getting stuck into a tureen of tepid brown tea.

I dropped the cigarette on the pavement and was just about to turn back in when a very large man stepped in front me, opened a knife and held it to my throat. Then he turned and came round next to me, facing the same direction, keeping the chill point pressed a wasp-sting's width into my skin. There was nobody around to see this.

'Don't move,' he said, coldly.

'OK,' I said quietly.

'Are you Julian Smattering?'

I said nothing, and he pressed the blade a millimetre further in.

'I said, are you—'

'Yes. Yes. Listen, please I don't have any money.'

'Shut up. Come with me. Don't make a fuss. Come with me. We're going for a ride.'

He took my upper right arm in his left and frogmarched me over to a Beamer parked around the corner. I got in the back with him. Finally we pulled up outside a grim pub somewhere off York Way, and the car and driver disappeared. My kidnapper accompanied me through the deserted public bar, where a woman averted her gaze from us as if from some poignant disfigurement. He curtly invited me to sit opposite a fat, hardfaced man at a table in the back room. There was a silence, broken by a metallic glissando of notes from the fruit machine in the corner.

'My name's Wigley,' this man said. 'And you are Julian Smattering, studying for a PhD on William Wordsworth. Is that right?'

'Yes. Look, how do you know that?'

'We have contacts.'

'But what the hell do you want from me? Can't you just let me go?'

'I'm afraid I can't do that, Julian. But I do have a proposition. How would you like to earn a hundred thousand pounds for a couple of hours' work?'

Glissando up. Glissando down. A motorbike outside in the street.

'What do you mean?'

'Well, look.' He eased himself forward and rested his elbows on the table. 'What do you know about The Prelude?'

'What do I know about it? It's Wordsworth's most famous poem, his autobiographical masterpiece, not published until after his death in 1850.'

'Not in full it wasn't,' said the man, with fascinating finality and confidence. 'I have in my possession the early manuscript, stolen in 1846, and in the hands of a private dealer in Dubai from whom it was, shall we say, taken by a third party and given to me. It contains the 550-line passage describing in explicit detail the drug-fuelled three-way conjugal congress that took place in Dove Cottage over thirty-six hours, between William, Annette Vallon, the eventual mother of his child, and

Princess Antoinette of Brunswick-Wolfenbüttel!'

I was stunned. The existence of the explicit sex in The Prelude had long been only a rumour in the Wordsworth scholarship community.

'Rubbish,' I said at last. 'It's a scam, a fake.'

Wigley pursed his lips, and smiled for the first time.

'Well,' he said. 'Why don't I show you a sample xerox?'

He opened the box, daintily removed a single leaf with finger and thumb and placed it down in front of me, turning it round so that I could read it. It was a photocopy of an A5-sized page. The date at the top was 1841. The handwriting was sloped and crabbed. I gasped. My hand shot to my mouth.

For Wordsworth scholars, this was the holy grail. The much whispered-about original version of The Prelude with the hardcore sexually explicit content. The writing blurred before my eyes. But it could not be by anyone but Wordsworth. My nerveless fingers dropped the page and I staggered out to the men's lavatory to be sick – with euphoria.

When I returned, Wigley had returned the pages to his box.

'All right,' I said quietly. 'I believe you. But what does this have to do with me?'

'Well, look,' he said. 'I want to sell this material. Potentially, it's the most valuable piece of property I've ever had. But as I understand it, there's only one possible buyer and that's someone in America. In Texas.'

'Do you mean the Harry Ransom Center in Austin, Texas?'

Wigley exchanged nods with his friend.

'Yeah. That's it. But they won't touch it if they think it's stolen. We have to find a way of persuading them that it's somehow got respectably lost all these years, and that the current owner is respectable. And that's where you come in.'

'Me?'

'Yes, you. We need you to convince these people in Texas that you've somehow blundered across it. That some library was just chucking it out. It's perfectly believable that you should get hold of it.'

I exhaled scornfully.

'No way. No way would the British Library have such a thing lying around, and not know what it was, and no way would they then just chuck it out. It's just not plausible.'

'Not the British Library. Keswick Public Library, near Dove Cottage in the Lake District. Next Wednesday, they're having a clearout of surplus stock: manky old paperbacks – that sort of thing. They're just selling them for something like 10p each to anyone who wants them.'

'So?'

'So you turn up, take some books, and then claim that this box of old papers was among the stuff they were throwing out.'

'What? How on earth would the Keswick Public Library have this?'

Wigley shrugged.

'Who knows? Who cares? Somehow, this cardboard box filled with papers got lost, and passed from pillar to post and ended up there, and no one knew how important it was. The only thing that matters is that you are now the legal owner. The respectable owner. So you have to get them to take money for it, to prove ownership. We could even let you do a bit of a press interview. Plucky young student, studying William Wordsworth, finds priceless Wordsworth three-way sex manuscripts. Then you sell them to this place in Texas. The price is secret, but you'll keep a hundred grand. The rest goes to us.'

Here, Wigley exchanged significant glances with his associate.

'And if I say no?'

Wigley's friend and the driver stood up and moved over to where I was standing.

'I know where you live,' was all he said.

This was 55b Dresden Road, in Archway, North London, the address to which I returned much later that night, having had a few drinks to seal the deal with my new friends, at the pub where we were talking and then later at a members' club in King's Cross.

'Hiya!' I said, as I crashed through the door, which bashed against the wall and shuddered back almost into my face. 'Hiya! We're rich! Rich! Hiya! Janine! Hi!' I sidled past our two bicycles in the hall, then up the stairs into our flat.

Janine was sitting with her back to me at the kitchen table, quite still.

'Hiya! Hiya! We're rich! I'm doing a special job for someone for eighty thousand quid!'

Janine twisted round to face me.

'Sorry I'm a bit late home.'

My eyes strayed to the clock, which disclosed that it was twenty to two in the morning.

'Yes. Look, I'm sorry. I'm late. But darling, I've got something incredible to tell you; today I made the most incredible discovery, and someone's offered me — us — eighty thousand pounds for just a few hours' work.'

Janine stood up, pale, imperious. She said nothing. For the first time, I noticed a packed suitcase near her feet. Her mobile rang; Janine answered it and said: 'Yes, I'll be right down.'

Then she turned to me.

'That's my Uber. I'm leaving you now, Julian. Leaving you for good. I've been offered a job as creative director at the Pret A Manger in Aberdeen. I'm sick of hearing about your stupid PhD on William Wordsworth. Sick of you personally, in fact. You come home at all hours, reeking of self-satisfaction and strong Czech lager. I'll send someone for my things later. Goodbye Julian. Goodbye for ever.'

She left. I listened to the cab take her up the street and away. I put the kettle on, opened the fridge, found a semi-wrapped block of cheddar and, holding it like a choc-ice, thoughtfully began to eat.

It was a cloudy day when I presented myself outside the public library in Keswick the following week. Various Lake District walkers in cagoules were trudging past, keen on a walk up to Helvellyn or Dolly Wagon Peak. There was a fine misty rain. On the library's glass door there was a sign: Surplus Stock For Sale. The arrangement was that I should be there by 11am, which is when the sale started, and wait.

It was now 11:22.

Suddenly a BMW pulled up, and Wigley's driver stuck his head out of the rear passenger window.

'C'm'ere!'

I went over, and he tried passing me the box out of the window, which was too small. Forcing it, he made a rip in the cardboard.

'For fuck's sake!'

'Just open up the door and pass it to me,' I said, mildly.

He did so.

'Right. There it is. Get in there, pick up some books, take them over to the woman at the front, with this box, and say this is what you want. Don't forget. Pay for them – and get a receipt.'

He roared away. I went into the library, hoping no one noticed what I was carrying in with me. There were a few people in there, browsing at the rows of old books on trestle tables. Someone looked up at me as I entered. Was he Special Branch? I scooped up two thrillers by Desmond Bagley, plonked them on top of my box and marched up to the woman at the front.

'I'd like to buy these please,' I said clearly and politely. 'These two books and this manuscript.'

'Just take them if you like,' she said, not looking up from her copy of *Grazia*. 'Take them.'

'No, I want to pay for them,' I said firmly.

For the first time, the woman frowned with puzzlement, and pointed to my box.

'Did you get that here?'

'Yes.'

She frowned again, and then shrugged, unable to summon any more interest in the matter.

'Well, if you really insist, you can give us a few quid.'

I smartly presented her with a crisp, ATM-fresh ten-pound note.

'Well, thank you sir,' she now said, humouring me. 'I'll make sure it goes to my supervisor.'

'Excellent. And now, could I have a receipt please? Could you write "for two books and one manuscript"?'

The woman stared at me, with irritation and astonishment. But she did as I asked, and five minutes later I was out of there.

Wigley's friend was supposed to meet me again at half past twelve, to get the box back, with the receipt. The arrangement was that they would have both for safe-keeping. But as I was hanging around, I felt the box start to collapse. It had been damaged when he had tried shoving it out of the car window and it was coming to pieces. The pages were actually falling out on to the pavement, but I rescued them, and transferred the whole stack to a plastic carrier bag I'd got earlier, buying a sandwich from a supermarket.

Suddenly, another of Wigley's associates turned up: the driver. He was on foot this time.

'Give it to me,' he hissed and, without letting me say anything, grabbed the empty box. Just as he felt the lack of weight, and was looking up at me questioningly, Wigley's other associate suddenly appeared, also on foot, shot a glance at the driver and then at me, then appeared to lunge at the man, his hand a silvery blur. He grabbed the box and ran off. The driver hunched over, clutching a spreading dampness on his shirt.

I clutched my Desmond Bagley books and could say nothing.

'Oh my God,' said a passerby. 'Oh no,' said someone else.

'Oh Jesus.' That was me. 'He's... He's not breathing.'

After a while, the police arrived. I had nothing to tell them.

Later that night, when I had got back to London, I saw on the television a news report about a contretemps involving the death of a petty criminal associated with notorious North London mobster Jake 'The Jakester' Wigley in the environs of Dove Cottage in the Lake District. Two photos flashed up on screen: Wigley's driver and Wigley himself. I looked over at the corner of the room, towards the carrier bag containing the manuscript of William Wordsworth's hugely long pornographic poem, 'The Prelude'.

I hadn't read it yet. I had things to think about. To alleviate my disquiet, I picked up one of the Desmond Bagley novels. Just to take my mind off things.

All that was a year ago. My thesis on Desmond Bagley is now complete. What a very remarkable and underrated author he is. I am abandoning my Wordsworth studies. I now see that research is a dead-end. As for the manuscript itself, I have put it away. I no longer care to pursue it. There can be no point in intervening further in the stale world of Wordsworth scholarship when my work on Desmond Bagley is bearing such fruit. The point is I am not a manuscript person. I'm an ideas person. A theory person. That is who I am. I have actually been offered a lectureship at Cambridge on the strength of my Bagley work.

Yet even now, with the rail ticket to Cambridge in my hand, I hesitate. The reason is that five minutes ago, my mobile rang.

'Mr Smattering?'

'Yes.'

'I think you are an acquaintance of my old friend Wigley?'

I said nothing, and after a moment, the voice continued.

'Tell me, Mr Smattering, what do you know about the manuscript of Lord Byron's memoirs?'

Then the line went dead. Bad mobile coverage. The number didn't come up on my phone. Perhaps he will call back. I keep the phone in my hand, staring at it. Finally, I sit down. The train can wait. Perhaps he will call back.

HOLINESS

Only creative reason can show us the way. That concept is what I have always lived by, and it is a modification, in fact a secularisation, of my mentor's great maxim, which in its entirety reads: 'Only creative reason, which in the crucified God is manifested as love, can really show us the way.' And it is in this spirit that I reflect on the events of the past few years – these words seem especially appropriate.

My first meeting with the late pontiff involved a crisis of protocol. Of course I knew that former US presidents must always be addressed as 'Mr President'. But how to address the emeritus Pope Benedict XVI, formerly Joseph Aloisius Ratzinger? Incredibly, it was not a problem that had occurred to me until we were brought face to face, near his residence, the Mater Ecclesiae Monastery in the Vatican Gardens. In my bewilderment, my stammering mortification, I instinctively truncated the traditional honorific, blurting out the single word 'Holiness' and making a deferential, slightly teutonic inclination of the head: a mannerism I stuck to in his presence after that. Something in this improvised form pleased him. He smiled. It was rare for him to do so.

I myself am not a cradle Catholic. My mother was a member of the Church of England, in which I was christened and confirmed in the conventional way. My father had no faith and used to joke: 'First time I was in church they threw water over me, second time confetti, and the third time, old boy, it will be earth!'

In fact he was cremated.

I went up to university in the late 1990s to read divinity and it was there that I found I enjoyed writing poetry. I had never actually had a girlfriend and was very shy, due to my ugly and absurd monobrow, a grotesque disfigurement that I had learned to live with. I was received into the church, and on graduating I became a teacher in a Catholic boys' school in the Midlands, but continued to publish poems, one of which emerged in a Catholic literary magazine. I can hardly remember the poem now. It was called 'Balance'. There was some imagery comparing the outstretched arms of Christ during the crucifixion to the level positioning of scales. A callow piece of work. I have all but forgotten it.

Yet something in this poem caught the attention of the Emeritus Pope. And it was when I was attending a conference for Catholic schoolteachers in Vatican City in 2012, that I was passed a note. A young priest appeared in the auditorium where I was hearing a lecture on the Neocatechumenal Way. He discreetly leaned from the aisle into the row where I was seated, and handed me a folded sheet of paper. Then he vanished.

This message gave me to understand that Benedict himself had read my poem, was aware of my attendance at the conference and wished to see me. It was an honour not to be taken lightly.

The hour of our meeting came at 5pm. I was to meet the former pontiff in the garden, and was conveyed into his presence by his private secretary, who withdrew as soon we caught sight of Benedictus, after signalling that I should continue to walk towards him alone. The man himself was seated under a plane tree, reading. I bowed, kissed the ring which he held out, and then sat in the chair opposite to which he gestured. At close quarters, I could see how silvery and silky his hair was, with that yellowy look that some old people's white hair gets. His skin itself was very unlined and the eyes fierce and clear.

'Where are you from, David?' he asked, with a surprisingly strong German accent. I replied: 'Newcastle in England... Holiness.'

'Ah,' returned Benedictus. 'The hometown of my old friend, Basil Hume. A great man.'

A brief silence settled on the conversation.

'I was very impressed by your poem, David,' he said at last, holding up what appeared to be a xerox. I was about to say how moved I was by his interest, when Benedictus held his hand up sharply, displeased by what he clearly felt was my shrill false modesty. 'And I should like you to read some creative work that I have written.' At this, he produced a bound volume of typewritten pages and gave them to me. 'Take this to your lodgings. Read it overnight, and come back here tomorrow at five, after your lectures. At that time, we can perhaps have some tea, and you can give me your honest opinion.' At this, he rang a small silver bell, which summoned the priest whom I had seen before. This young man appeared instantly, and I was silently given to understand that I should go with him. I tried to say some sort of farewell, but Benedictus was already looking away from me, reading a Bible bound in white calf, and he did not acknowledge my departure.

Only after an unbearably tense two hours of lectures was I permitted to return to my tiny cell-like room, and open the document that His Holiness had given me. What on earth could it be? An epic poem? A novel?

At first, I thought that it was a play. But no. What I took to be stage directions were written all in capitals, and though the dialogue was aligned to the left margin in the normal way, the character names for each speech cue were centred on the page. There were phrases like 'C/U' and 'INT. NIGHT'.

Benedictus XVI had written a screenplay. The first scene, over the credits, apparently showed the exterior of an American high school. There were to be swarms of teenage boys and girls going up the steps into the building: evidently the beginning of a school day. All expensively dressed. Some truant groups were lackadaisically hanging about to the side, some boys speaking flirtatiously to girls, some throwing frisbees, some furtively using soft drugs. All these details His Holiness had specified, along with a pop song on the soundtrack: Avril Lavigne's 'Sk8er Boi'.

Then the camera was to pick out two particular characters: twin boys – His Holiness described them as 'hotties' – dressed far less expensively than the others, carrying skateboards, looking nervous and trying ingratiating little smiles at the young people who were to be their fellow pupils. The next shot was to be these boys' own point of view: various fellow pupils staring directly at them, catching the camera's gaze briefly, with expressions of derision or incredulity, but parting to let them through as the boys move towards the steps.

I was only two pages into the script but I just had to set it down on the bare desk at which I was sitting, next to my spartan single bed, and place my hand on my forehead. A hot dizziness all but overwhelmed me. What could His Holiness mean by this? I flipped back to the beginning and for the first time read the title page: DOUBLE TROUBLE.

In the bottom left-hand corner of the page was His Holiness's own name, Benedict XVI, and his Vatican address. There was a single landline telephone number.

Thoughtfully, I left the manuscript where it was, walked over to the open window and looked out onto the hot Roman night. The thought of reading the entire text daunted me more than anything in my life: I remembered the feeling I used to have as an undergraduate when I was about to embark for the first time on Augustine's *Confessions* or Thomas a Kempis's *The Imitation of Christ*. The same anticipation that a mountaineer must feel, lacing on his boots at base camp. I took a deep breath and returned to my desk, carrying a glass of water with me, and continued to read.

After an hour and a half, I was finished: in every sense. I was emotionally exhausted. Wrung out. I had laughed, I had cried, I had gasped with astonishment, and at the climactic scenes I had literally risen from the chair with my fists above my head and cried out: 'Yes! Yes! YES!' — so audibly that there were derisive replying calls from the street outside.

It was a remarkable story. The two twins, named Caleb and Ethan, were new arrivals, having been homeschooled by their parents until the age of fifteen. One was brilliant at science and naturally successful with girls, the other gifted at humanities and hopeless with girls, and with an unsightly monobrow, very similar to mine: a veritable giant caterpillar above his eyes. But Caleb, the scientific one, invents a pheremone after school in the chemistry lab which makes people irresistible to the opposite sex. It has the effect of making the headmistress or 'principal', Mrs Golobiowski, fall in love with Ethan, and she is the mother of Julie, the girl who has started dating Caleb.

What an uproarious situation!

But now Caleb reveals that the chief ingredient for the antidote to his pheremone is a phial of human tears of genuine sorrow for another's misfortune. Physical pain or self-pity will not do. So he contrives a situation in which Ethan tells Mrs Golobiowski about the death of his mother the previous month – which is incidentally the reason why their homeschooling has come to an end – and she begins to cry. Ethan thoughtfully dabs the tears away with a handkerchief, conveys the damp article to Caleb who wrings it into an eyedropper and decants the precious substance into her morning coffee. Her condition is cured. Meanwhile, Julie's own twin sister Helen has heard Ethan's story, having been passing the corridor at the time, and fallen in love with him out of compassion. There is a double wedding scene. Credits – and then His Holiness had contrived an amusing 'post-credits sting' during which the school's ageing, hideous janitor is shown curiously dabbing some of the pheremone on himself, with a gorgeous blonde cheerleader about to meet him in the corridor.

The following afternoon I met His Holiness in a state of high excitement.

'So. What are your views?' he rasped in his deep German

accent, without any preamble, as I sat down and placed his manuscript on the table.

'Well, Holiness,' I said, a little breathless, 'I think it's lovely, almost Shakesp—'

'No, no,' he said impatiently. 'I mean what are your views on casting?'

I was nonplussed: 'Well, I don't really—'

'I'm thinking Susan Sarandon for Mrs Golobiowski,' he said. 'What do you think?'

'I…that…'

He looked at me shrewdly. 'You think there might be an availability issue? You could be right.'

He sipped his tea.

'And the twins? Who do you like for the twins?'

My mouth opened soundlessly, goldfish-style, and His Holiness went on speaking, his voice gaining a deeper and more gravelly severity: 'I think the Paul twins. Logan and Jake. You realise they are completely massive on YouTube?'

Again, I could not think of anything to say, and again His Holiness directed a piercing glance at me, displeased, but evidently respecting the courage I was showing in disagreeing with his view.

'You worry that they have no experience in acting?'

'Well, I —'

'But that is just the point. They have no experience in acting and that is precisely what gives us an advantage when it comes to negotiating their fee. And of course in dealing with them on location. Of course much of that is down to the director. I was thinking Patty Jenkins would have a real feel for the material.'

He leant back, nodding slowly and sagely. 'Anyway,' he said. 'Take this script and shop it around town. Trust me. They'll be biting our hands off for this one.' He dismissed me with a flick of the hand and returned to read his calf-bound Bible. But while I was walking away he called me back with a guttural throat-clearing grunt, and said: 'There is something else. I was thinking of playing the janitor myself.' He met my stupefied gaze briefly, and then with a lift of the chin silently dismissed me again.

I had to leave for home that afternoon. The screenplay was in my hand luggage as I boarded the flight and never left my side in the days and weeks to come. On my return to London I could think of nothing more than to send the script to an old university contemporary of mine, now working in television, with whom I was acquainted on Facebook. I excised the author's name from the title page, scanned it into my MacBook Air and emailed it over to him, with a rather sheepish covering note. The response came with staggering swiftness. My friend had shown the screenplay to a colleague of his, a producer in Los Angeles, who apparently simply went mad for it.

'There is no author name on the coversheet. Is it you? I bet it's you. You dark horse!' I could say nothing, other than to agree on a meeting in London when his contact was over briefly.

'I think we can get Donald Sutherland for the janitor!' this man said excitedly at the beginning of our discussion, as the three of us sat at one end of a large polished conference table, adorned with bowls of jelly babies, and film posters up on the walls. He added: 'With Donald Sutherland in the picture, we can get all sorts of Canadian funding. Sutherland's a lock!'

Something in my face must have alarmed them, because my friend said: 'You had someone else in mind for the caretaker?'

'Ah, no.'

'No one?'

'No.'

'No-one at all?'

'No.'

The meeting concluded amiably enough. I telephoned His Holiness' office repeatedly but was unable to get through to him, unable to ask if he was content to let the production go ahead on this basis. I assumed he might want to use a pseudonym, so I let my own name go on the credits. My fee was enormous. I tried to find some way of forwarding the money to His Holiness but there seemed no way of achieving this.

When the final day of principal photography came around, we were on location in Vancouver and the time came to shoot the credit-sting scene with Donald Sutherland, the only star name we had managed to attract. But just as we were all set up, my friend – now the executive producer – scurried up and whispered intently that Sutherland had fallen sick and all the Canadian funding had fallen through. But the good news was that there had been new tranche of cash from German and Italian sources, contingent on 'new casting'. Round the corner, in janitor's uniform, and carrying a steel bucket and mop, came Benedict XVI, his face set in a very grim expression.

'Holiness!' I couldn't help myself saying it, but he refused to meet my eye; he walked on past me, his steel bucket clanging.

His scene was not a success. Our teenage cheerleader tried gamely to impersonate someone who would find him attractive in some sort of absurdly drugged state. But His Holiness simply refused to perform the moment where he had to run away from her. He just stood there, fixing his young co-star with a piercing stare.

The film itself was released straight to download and His Holiness was not credited – and not recognised. It came out under a different title. I am reluctant to say which. But it continues to be a commercial success and I have always donated my income direct to a Catholic charity, though His Holiness himself rebuffed any attempts at contact. My guilt and shame were almost unbearable.

Then, one week ago, as advent season began, I made a decision to renounce my worldly existence, to give all my money and goods away and live austerely at a monastery in a remote corner of Belgium. And just as I was making the final donation online, a strange and wonderful thing happened. Nothing less than a Christmas miracle. I could feel tiny hairs fall from above the bridge of my nose and they showered like cherry blossom in a sudden breeze. A mass of little black flecks, like a murmuration of starlings falling through the air. The pattern those hairs made on my computer keyboard was a depiction of divine grace. I got up and looked into my bathroom mirror.

My monobrow had gone. Touching the exposed skin I felt a smoothness that no shaving or waxing had ever been able to achieve. I felt whole again. And the blessed duality and balance of those eyebrows would always remind me of His Holiness' great work. And its original title.

ALL THIS AGGRAVATION

I entered Government service in the Bicentennial year. That was fitting. Met two gentlemen from the National Security Agency at a coffee shop in the Hilton Hotel, Las Vegas, formerly the International, right next to the showroom. They said they would be willing to overlook my federal tax liability in exchange for assistance. Would that be acceptable, they asked? I replied: hell, yes it would be acceptable. Not only that, it was what I was already doing. I was already supplying information to the Government. I had met with the President himself. So I was already being of assistance.

Those boys finished up their coffee and left, and I went back to my suite. Soon I received a letter from the IRS informing me that a recent review of the situation had been settled in my favour, like they say in Monopoly. But soon after that I got a call late at night from some guy saying that I had to kill someone.

Have you ever had to do that? And I mean not like fighting in a war or anything but actually kill someone in civilian life. I never had. A guy I knew who was a bodyguard back in the early 1960s told me he had. He said the first time it was like when you get lucky away at some convention and cheat on your wife with a real knockout twenty years younger than you. You wake up next morning, all alone back in your hotel room, and you kind of can't believe it actually happened and it wasn't just imaginary. Well, it was like that. After the job's finished, with no problems, you can't believe it, you can't believe it actually happened, you killed someone, and here you are, back again, living your life, back the same as before.

The man I had to kill was called Al Bramlet. He was a labour union leader. Rich guy. Actually owned a company himself, that made shelves. Seriously. Shelves. Sold shelves to hotels and casinos. Sold shelves to businesses that put plates and stuff on the shelves. Not, like, just planks of wood; they had little metal brackets and so on, but even so. Also, he owned the asses of three hundred thousand workers in Las Vegas: chefs, captains, bartenders, valets, even croupiers. All these people paid union dues and Bramlet took his personal cut from those in the form of expenses. Certain bars and restaurants had started employing non-union labour and undercutting agreed rates. If that kind of thing goes unpunished, figures Mr Bramlet, then pretty soon confidence in the existing arrangement becomes undermined, and pretty soon after that his income goes into the toilet and he has to rely on shelves.

Bramlet had started planting bombs in the non-union restaurants and bars, actual bombs. Small bombs. Or actually he paid a couple of other guys to do this – specialists. The bombs were threats. Sending a message. The agents were back telling me this stuff, incidentally, not in the hotel coffee shop this time but in a Denny's on South Maryland Parkway. We all of us were wearing baseball caps so as not to attract attention.

Some of the bombs hadn't gone off. People were discovering ticking packages in trash cans wrapped in black duct tape and calling the cops. Non-exploding bombs were making Bramlet look like a major asshole and he was getting into a serious beef with the guys who still wanted payment for their faulty explosives, and naturally these were connected guys. This whole dispute could escalate, and some of these gentlemen's association with the Nevada Gaming Commission and the Las Vegas Police Department could come to light. So the Government needed Al Bramlet shut down; they said it would look like it was the bomb guys who did it. But they still needed me actually to complete the business.

Now, I had guns in my possession and at my personal disposal. With permits. I had a Smith & Wesson Model 19, which I carried around with me, and a reliable snubnose Colt, and also some assault rifles back at my Tennessee residence. Used to get out to the firing range on Highland Avenue a little bit in those days and always got some very gratifying VIP service.

Figured I would use the Colt, but it turns out I couldn't discuss minutiae like this with the agents, who didn't want to know the details. Months went by without me hearing from them. Then, after Christmas, they told me to wait in the parking lot of McCarran Airport on a certain date in February 1977, and wait for Bramlet by his car. He was coming in off a flight from Reno. He wouldn't be armed. They told me the make and registration of his vehicle, and the time to be there.

Said I had to wait by the car, just standing around, which was kind of awkward. Supposing someone made me? You know – recognised me? They said just do it.

It was a pretty cold night. I wore a thick belted overcoat with scarf. The Colt was jammed in the right pocket. Didn't wear a glove on that hand. Kept leaving the gun in my coat with the safety on while I blew into my hand for warmth. Wore a cowboy hat so I wouldn't get recognised.

Bramlet showed up at twenty to twelve. The parking lot was deserted. He shouted out: 'Hey, what you doing?' when he saw me standing by the car, but close to, he knew who I was and he was surprised to see me. He used my Christian name, which I dislike. We had never met, never been introduced. I took out the Colt, pointed it at him, told him to get in the car and he was going to take me for a drive out to the desert.

'You fat fuck,' he said. 'You fat fuck.'

'Just get in.'

'Fuck you, you fat fuck.'

'In the car.'

Once we were out in the desert, we stopped at a payphone, just like I'd agreed with the agents, and told him to make a call, borrow some money, to pay off the guys who made the bombs. Bramlet nodded like he knew the score, and he looked a lot less angry and scared. He even smiled. He said something about how I knew everyone in this town, and I smiled too and said it was true.

We got out of the car together. Bramlet actually had a roll of quarters cased in grey paper, from the bank, a heavy-looking tube of coins. At first I'd thought it was a cigar or something. He spoke to someone and I heard him say: 'Ten grand will be no problem.' Eventually he hung up the receiver and gave it a little pat, for my benefit I guess, to show how everything was jake.

He turned around and the next thing he was calling me by my Christian name again, which I don't like, and then he asked: 'Could I have an autograph? You know, for my—'

I shot him in the face, and in the chest. The first bullet caused his cheek to sort of collapse and his mouth kind of rode up like he was tasting something sour, and exposed a row of teeth. The second two shots made him slump back against the phone and slide down. He still had the roll of quarters with the paper ripped and I took those and put them in my pocket. It wasn't until a few seconds after that that I thought to check that nobody was around, but nobody was.

Rolling the guy on to his stomach, I pretty well got hold of his shirt up at the neck and his belt and heaved him into this ditch behind the payphone that was supposed to be there and kicked some rocks on to him. By this time, I was feeling some sharp pains in my chest and up my arm and I saw light-flashes like fireflies.

Got back behind the wheel and drove home; cancelled a couple of shows; even cancelled breakfast that first day back.

Checked the papers every day after that. Nothing for a good long while. Then I saw something about Al Bramlet's body being found and stuff about labour disputes and organised crime. Almost a month later, two police officers came by the hotel and asked if I had ever met Al Bramlet. I said no, signed some autographs and they left but I got the chest pains and light-flashes back again. And it was then that the two NSA guys came to me with a new offer.

There was a problem, they said. There was a problem and there was nothing to be done. It hadn't gone as smoothly as they'd hoped. Long story short: I could do hard time – for the murder, or for tax evasion. It wouldn't go so well for me in prison, they said. I would have a target painted on my ass. The hell is that supposed to mean, I shouted, standing up. But there they were again – the chest pains, light-flashes – and I had to calm down.

The new plan was that they would make it all go away by faking my death over the summer, sometime in August. With a heart attack in the residence at Tennessee. I would succumb to a tragic heart attack seated on the toilet upstairs. Fake body in the coffin, and then with a whole new identity I would start my new life in Biloxi, Mississippi. I asked: but how do I sing? How do I make music? How do I make movies? You don't, they said, but on the other hand, you don't get sodomised in the shower in Carson City penitentiary every day of your natural-born life – so it's your choice.

Actually got set up in the house in Biloxi for a solid week before the news broke. All those flowers and people. Very moving.

Thought I would miss music, but I never did. I listen to a lot of gospel on the radio. Hum along some. Brought a guitar with me from Memphis, but Lord knows, strumming that thing was never the strong suit on my best day. It just lies there. Get up around ten, eat Cheerios with milk. Go out a little before lunch. Don't drive. Walking is better for me, and the strangest thing is that I actually lost weight. Little bit. Stop by the bank to pick up the cash allowance the agency sends me. Some groceries. Newspaper. Still take Quaaludes – that's something else the agency organised: on prescription, no questions.

I've been walking out with a neighbour lady who is a widow. She is called Mary, and she calls me Aaron. We sometimes sit on her back porch, hand in hand. She has an ice tea and I have a beer, or sometimes ice tea as well. The afternoons are kind of a siesta situation. Shouldn't really. Makes sleeping at night so damn difficult but this is what happens.

One thing I took with me from Memphis: the Colt. I don't know if the agency know about this. But anyway I took the Colt and six boxes of ammo. Get out in the yard every once in a while, set up a couple of empty beer bottles on crates, take aim, keep my hand in. Stay sharp.

TAKE OFF

I never liked card games. I'm awful at whist. I can't manage bridge, and as a child, snap made me cry because I used to think something had broken. But Daddy was a great poker player and he told me something that I have always remembered. There's always a chump in a poker game, he said – someone destined to be cleaned out. Look around at your fellow players, and if you can't spot the chump...then it's you.

I'm acting on tour with a new production of Agatha Christie's *A Murder Is Announced*. We're going everywhere from the Theatre Royal Bury St Edmunds to the Liverpool Empire. I play the rather haughty cousin of Laetita Blacklock, the lady in whose house a terribly mysterious shooting occurs. I come on just before the interval, saying things like 'Well really!' and 'Cigarette?' For Miss Marple, we've got Natasha Sopel, who you probably won't remember. She played the overworked hospital consultant on *Holby City*, for years. Not that I'm knocking *Holby City*. I was on it once, playing the anguished middle-class parent of a fifteen-year-old who's brought in after a near-fatal car accident, and they find drug paraphernalia in his jeans pocket. Quite ridiculous of course, but it was a job and I was glad of the work. I wouldn't mind a nice telly now. Still. This tour is fun and I've been having an adventure.

There's a chap in the cast called Zeke. Insufferable name, but there we are. He's playing the cynical young writer character. Few years out of drama school. He's actually about twenty-six, twelve years younger than me. Supposedly got this girlfriend back in London but, as we say in the theatre, it doesn't count on tour. One night in Plymouth after the show, the cast got very drunk in the bar. We were staying at the Holiday Inn Express on internet discount rates. He walked me back to my room and one thing led to another.

Now I say twelve years younger than me, but that's not quite true. I told him I was thirty-eight, but I'm actually forty-three. White lie. He said he thought I was in my mid-thirties when we first had a drink which was rather sweet of him. I, being faux-modest, admitted to late thirties. I made up some nonsense about being thirty-eight on Valentine's Day. Now I'm stuck with it.

It's so funny. It's not that he's young and it's not that he's particularly handsome – because he's not, really. The thing that makes Zeke attractive is that he does impressions. Really. He does these voices. It's incredible. When we first had a drink, he impersonated Danny Lepage, our director. It was brilliant. He did the voice and the silly dynamic walk he does when he comes into the rehearsal room and throws his leather jacket down into the corner. Silly old queen. Zeke had me in stitches doing it. He did everyone else in the cast. It was incredible, and sort of eerie, and sort of exciting. I think I knew I was going to have a fling with him from the very moment I heard him do someone else's voice. Why is it so fascinating?

I challenged him to do the waiter's voice in a restaurant where we were having lunch. He did it. I challenged him to do the lady in the box office at Northampton, and he did it. He even did her funny walk. One night in my room, he did a wicked send-up of what Natasha would sound like having an orgasm, like a dolphin singing *The Mikado,* and I said to him, 'Zeke, you monster, is there anyone you can't do?' And he just grinned and shook his head and we had the best sex ever.

The next morning, I found Zeke had gone. He likes to go back to his own room after I've gone to sleep. But just lying there I had the strangest thought. I wonder if Zeke ever impersonates me? I suppose not. I'm far too dull and colourless to impersonate. I'm just me. I don't have any distinguishing characteristics, particularly. Not like these other people.

Still. It would be odd if I was the only person in the cast that he never ever impersonated, wouldn't it? We had coffee after the last show in our run at the Oxford Playhouse, and I almost made up my mind to ask him if he had ever done an impression of me. But somehow, I couldn't force the conversation that way. He kept talking about other people. I finally asked what he thought about the way I walked. 'Very alluring, darling' was all he would say.

I brooded about it all the way through the following week. I caught his eye in the wings just before we were about to go on – and then looked away. I didn't take his call during the day, and then later, when I called him, he apparently had his phone off. And then, after one show, I came into the pub and saw Zeke talking to all the rest of the cast and he seemed to be saying something in a very concerted way, and he broke off very guiltily when I broke in and said hello and everyone else looked very sheepish.

'What are we all discussing?' I asked brightly. 'Oh nothing; nothing much,' said Zeke, 'we were just talking about voiceovers. How very lucrative they are. I'm surprised you don't go in for a bit more voiceover work, darling!'

Normally, I'd love it if Zeke called me 'darling' in public. I'd love it if there was a public display of affection. But this just seemed dismissive. He went to the bar to get me a drink and I did what I've always done when someone is horrible to me in front of lots of people – I try to pretend it's some big in-joke – so I rolled my eyes for everyone's benefit and they all smiled.

The next few weeks, I became more and more obsessive. I would spend long minutes every morning looking at myself in the mirror, running my lines. Doing little vocal exercises. Screwing up my eyes, which has the effect of minimising my eye-bags while blurring my vision so I can't really see them as well. I really looked at myself. Occasionally, just while I was alone, looking in the mirror, I tried doing an impression of Zeke's voice. I just couldn't do it. It was just my voice, saying something that he might say. I had no idea how he saw himself. I had no idea how the people he impersonated saw themselves. Did they know they were doing all these strange little things, things out of the ordinary, that people could impersonate?

Then two weeks ago something extraordinary happened. Barry Fulwell, who plays the Inspector, spent too long in the pub before our first matinee in Lincoln and the silly sod fell over coming on. Twisted his ankle. He just about made it to the end of the show, but it only became worse and he got some sort of infection and temperature. There was no doubt about it, he couldn't do the rest of the run and there wasn't even a proper understudy.

So Zeke volunteered. He phoned Danny Lepage in London and told him he knew the lines and he could do it – and he could get some drama school chum to fill in his role which, God knows, was pretty undemanding. At first Danny was unconvinced. So were we all. The Inspector is a much older character, but Danny came up on the next train and Zeke did this incredible audition for him – basically a pitch-perfect impersonation of the way Barry did it. He sounded and moved like an older man. And the fact that he was doing an impression gave the whole thing a kind of dreamy, surreal quality. 'All right!' said Danny. 'You're on!'

We only had to cancel one performance before Zeke started. He was a triumph. The audience went mad for him, and a big London agent came round to his dressing room afterwards. I was actually in the room when that happened, and Zeke sort of had to give me a look to say he'd rather talk to the chap in private. Afterwards, when we were in bed, he did this very funny impression of him.

So the tour went on. We had a brief break for Christmas. I was on my own with my mother and he was back in London, presumably with his girlfriend, although it was just impossible for me to talk about that with him. In the New Year, we started all over again in Southampton and he was getting wonderful notices. Everything was right between us, but more and more often, he couldn't be with me, because he had to have dinner with some potential agent or manager, or he had to meet a bunch of his old mates from drama school, including the chap he'd dragooned into taking over his role.

He seemed just as affectionate, but I just got more and more obsessed with the idea that he was impersonating me behind my back. I would listen at the door of his dressing room when he had people in there. I would arrange to meet him and a couple of other people in the cast for a coffee or for lunch, and then arrive deliberately late, and try hanging back to overhear what they were saying. I even tried something I heard about on TV: I accidentally left my smartphone behind with the voice recorder on so that I could hear if Zeke was impersonating me.

But there was nothing. It just got worse and worse, and the more I suspected him, the more impossible it was to ask him about it flat out. But I knew he was doing something. He was always talking with these people and breaking off when he saw me coming, with this silly guilty grin on his face.

Things came to a head a week or so into February, when he said he wanted to have dinner. When I arrived – late as usual – he was surrounded by everyone. I heard him say my name and I just couldn't stand it any more.

'Zeke!' I shouted, storming up to the table. 'I know you're doing an impression of me, you absolute bastard. I know you doing a nasty impression of me behind my back. I know that's what you're doing. Well you can bugger off.'

There was silence and then everyone including Zeke backed away from the table and there was an enormous birthday cake with my name on it, and what looked thirty-eight candles.

'Happy birthday dearest,' he finally said in a teeny-tiny little voice. 'And happy Valentine's Day.'

Thirty-eight years old. That is what I am.

APPROPRIATION

The fetish market in Cotonou was a place Jacqueline generally disdained to visit. It was for tourists, undesirables, backpackers, foreigners who chose to see Benin as some exotic place and incidentally persisted with the intolerable Western condescension of calling Ganvié the 'Venice of Africa'. Absurd! Yet on that terrible day, Jacqueline found herself walking from the family home in the Cocotiers suburb into the centre of the city rather than taking her stylish little *moto*, walking in the fierce heat. Why? To test herself somehow?

She approached the *Grand Marché* from the West, and walked by the fetish stalls, where she bought a piece of wood which had been painted grey and whittled into an ambiguous tapering shape. Then she took a taxi back to the Government building where her father was employed, near the American Embassy: the Ministry of Economy and Finance. Jacqueline walked through the airy, angular lobby, her heels clattering on its cool stone floor, showed her laminated badge to the receptionist – she kept it on its lanyard in her bag – and knowing from long experience that there was no point in waiting for the lift, she walked up a single flight of stairs to where her father's office was to be found on the first floor.

Looking back on the events of that morning, now many years ago, Jacqueline often wondered how it was that nobody noticed anything wrong, nobody heard anything. She approached her father's outer office, preparing to chat with his assistant, Madame Mende. But Madame Mende was not there. Dust motes circled in the air, sparkling like points of light, almost reflected in the glass-fronted mahogany cabinets, which contained heavy volumes relating to export statistics. The door to her father's sanctum was ajar.

Jacqueline looked around, puzzled. It would be an error of taste and decorum to walk right in, without speaking to her father's subordinate staff, but there seemed nobody about. Moreover, he usually sensed her presence straight away and would welcome her with a cheerfully boisterous shout.

Not today. Jacqueline tapped hesitantly on the open door, pushing it open a little more and called out:

'Papa?'

She entered and immediately saw that her father was seated at his desk with his head down on its surface, near the expansive green blotter and dagger-shaped letter opener. His left hand dangled down at his side and the other rested on the desk. Near it, was his army service revolver. By his left ear, Jacqueline saw what she thought at first was a very large reddish fan, opened, its circular edge drooping over the edge of the desk, as if in a painting by Dalí.

She smelt the air, gave a little gasp, tried to cry or shriek, found she could not, and for a moment wheeled back into the secretarial antechamber to recover herself.

Some minutes passed. Jacqueline stumbled to the ladies' room down the hall and splashed some cold water on her face, and slurped a little from the tap. Then she walked back. Everywhere there was an eerie silence. She took a deep breath and re-entered her late father's office.

For the first time, she noticed that there was something else on his desk: a sealed white envelope on which was the word 'Jacqueline' in his handwriting. She took the letter; sickeningly, she had to slide it out from under his nerveless fingers. Now in a state of pure shock, she walked back out of the office, stuffing the envelope into her bag. She did not reply to the receptionist's farewell as she left the building and hailed a taxi outside on the street.

Jacqueline's mother took the news with her habitual intimidating calm. With the long elegant fingers of one hand splayed on her chest and the other hand over her mouth, she sat down silently on the floral couch in their lounge. Jacqueline produced the letter and showed it to her. Her mother simply nodded, as if to say: open it. If she was hurt or angered that her late husband had only addressed this to her daughter, she betrayed nothing.

The letter read as follows:

My dear Jacqueline,

By the time you read this, I will have passed to my reward. You and your mother must be strong, for my sake.

Enclosed with this letter I hereby give you the online usernames and passwords for my accounts at the Banque Atlantique Bénin and the Société Générale de Banques au Bénin. You will find there approximately 100,750,000,000

*CFA Francs. I do not care to go into the details, but this is
the accumulation of some informal consultancy fees I have
received. Once the news of my demise is officially released –
and especially the circumstances – the authorities may well
take action to distrain these accounts and any monies therein.
I advise you therefore to expatriate the funds to an account in
Europe as soon as possible.*

You and your mother will therefore be well cared for.

Papa

Jacqueline looked at her mother, who simply looked
impassively away, at the stand of lime trees visible from the
picture window.

'Expatriate the funds, *maman*? What on earth does that
mean?'

At that moment, the landline telephone rang piercingly,
and Jacqueline's mother gave another of her curt nods, as if
to say: answer it.

Madame Mende was on the line, hysterical with fear
and grief. She must have returned to the building just after
Jacqueline had left, having had her lunch at the corner café.
She discovered the body, and immediately called the police.
It occurred to Jacqueline part-way through their conversation
that she should be pretending to be hearing the news for the
first time, but Madame Mende was far too distraught to notice
anything inconsistent in her behaviour. Eventually, Jacqueline
was able to bring the nerve-jangling exchange to an end. She
turned to her mother, who had been listening and understood
Jacqueline's dissimulation. At that moment, they heard the
engine of an approaching police car, and the merest glance
between them sealed their mutual decision to behave as if they

had just learned everything from Madame Mende. Jacqueline returned the letter and its torn envelope to her bag, just as the doorbell rang.

After the police had left, Jacqueline and her mother made the decision to widen the circle of trust to include Jacqueline's fiancé Etienne, an employee of the fisheries division, who joined them later that day for a simple supper of consommé in elegant large white china bowls. an ascetic salad and a jug of cold tap water, served by their maid Ode, who withdrew once the food was on the table.

The delicately administered kiss on both cheeks that Etienne gave his future mother-in-law on arrival spoke much. He had never presumed such familiarities before, and thus mutely signalled that Jacqueline had brought him entirely up to speed about the existence and contents of her father's note.

'He was right, of course,' said Etienne, once Ode had cleared everything away and vanished. 'The money should be transferred to a European account. In fact, I suggest the UK. I also suggest that you begin to look for some residential property in London.'

'I will open an account tomorrow morning,' said Jacqueline.

'No,' warned Etienne. 'Such a thing would only alert the authorities.'

'What, then?' asked Jacqueline's mother sharply.

'We will have to find a complaisant British account holder to accept the money *pro tem*. Do you know of one?'

Baffled and slightly affronted, both women shook their heads.

'Then we frankly have a problem, and time is running out. It can't be long before the *Sûreté Nationale* demands access to these accounts. There is only one thing that I can suggest. We approach a British subject at random and ask him if we can deposit our money in his bank account for a few months, in return for which we will offer him ten per cent of the total.'

'Have you taken leave of your senses?' snapped Jacqueline's mother so fiercely that Ode, who had entered with the coffee, simply turned on her heel and returned with her full tray to the kitchen.

'Eight per cent,' said Etienne, placatingly.

Jacqueline's mother waved this angrily away. 'That is not what I meant. This British person will cheat us. He will do what the British have always done here. He will rob us. He will appropriate all our money and there is nothing we can do to stop this appropriation.'

Etienne shrugged. 'It is a risk, yes. But it is the only thing we can do to show the authorities that we do not have the money. I will send an email to a British internet account and we will see what happens.'

Without another word, Etienne stood – and Jacqueline stood also – and the couple led the way to Jacqueline's bedroom, where her laptop stood ready. Jacqueline's mother was too tense, and now too fatalistically resigned, to notice that this plan must also have been something that Etienne and Jacqueline had discussed between themselves.

Etienne sat down and painstakingly typed the following, as the two women peered over his shoulder.

From: etiennegrave@gouv.bj
To: johnsmith@btinternet.com
Dear Mr Smith, please allow me to introduce myself, and I take this opportunity to address myself to you in the love of

Jesus Christ. My name is Etienne Grave and I am the future son-in-law of the late minister of mines in Cotonou in Benin. Due to various factors liable to be misinterpreted by the police in this country, M. D'Sang was in receipt of the equivalent of 130,000,000 English pounds. M. D'Sang's relations are now intending to leave the country and it is imperative that we have a safe UK account in which this money is placed while they remove themselves from Benin. We need a safe, honourable and honest person to hold this money for us for the time being. If you send me your bank account details we can arrange for the money to be put in your account and then moved on, in return for which we are prepared to give you eight per cent of the total as your fee. Please email me back with these details as soon as possible.

Yours in Christ, E. Grave

Etienne pressed the 'send' button and there was a tense, solemn silence.

'We can only pray that this John Smith helps us, and that he is honest, and that he does not simply appropriate everything,' said Jacqueline's mother quietly. The others nodded.

At the funeral the following day, Jacqueline, her mother and Etienne sat together in church, intensely aware of the deceased's apparent friends and colleagues crowding behind them in large numbers. Madame Mende was accorded the honour of sitting next to the widow. Many – in fact the overwhelming majority – were people they had never seen before. These men were evidently his professional contacts and associates, some from neighbouring states. Jacqueline uneasily wondered: did these people consider themselves to be her father's creditors, in some way? And at the back stood many in suits and dark glasses: officers of the *Sûreté Nationale* perhaps. At the wake afterwards, many guests pressed their cards on her and her mother, and asked if they could have meetings. The two women were able to use their grief as an excuse to avoid agreeing to a date and time.

That entire morning of course, they could think of nothing but Mr Smith from England and whether he would help them. Once their guests had all gone, the three of them went straight to Jacqueline's bedroom to look at the email messages on her laptop. They could hardly suppress their excitement on discovering that there was a reply, and Jacqueline was astonished to hear her mother quietly whisper the word *merde*.

From: johnsmith@btinternet.com
To: etiennegrave@gouv.bj

Dear Mr Grave,

Many thanks for your email. I was very surprised to receive it. But I certainly want to be of assistance to you if I can. I have discussed this matter with my wife and we have agreed that we can help. My bank account details are 20-83-36 (sort code) and 54132309 (account number). The only question I have is: when would your money arrive in my account? And when would you want me to transfer it to another account, minus my eight per cent? (Although I should point out that this would represent my gross gain; there would be a considerable liability vis-à-vis capital gains tax).

Yours ever, John Smith

Jacqueline gave a little skip of delight and Etienne a tiny fist pump. 'Yes!' he hissed. 'The first phase of our plan is complete.

Thank heavens for this Mr Smith. I am certain that we can trust him.'

It was at this point that Jacqueline and Etienne considered whether Etienne should simply return to his own apartment in Cocotiers, or whether he might, under the circumstances, stay the night. Their wedding date had been fixed for three months' time but they had not yet had full relations. Jacqueline's mother tactfully withdrew, and with a sort of roguish daring, Etienne took Jacqueline's hand and led her into her bedroom, closed the door, theatrically placed a forefinger on his lips and turned off the light. After fifteen minutes, Jacqueline understood that this phase of their relationship was now at an end; it evidently pleased Etienne in the course of their love-play to strike his fiancée with his closed fist, this being indispensable to achieving his erection, and then climactically hissing into her ear that both the money, and an intimate part of her anatomy were 'his'. Then Jacqueline felt his full weight relax upon her and then, in the darkness, heard him snore.

She stared dully at the ceiling and it was many hours before she could get to sleep.

But just when everything seemed to be going smoothly with their arrangements... Disaster. Jacqueline walked into her mother's lounge area, where she was discussing with her future son-in-law the relative merits of Reigate and Redhill, and announced: 'We have a problem. I was at the bank this morning and the manager wanted to see me. I think he might be aware of our circumstances. Before he will release Daddy's money into Mr Smith's account, he wants... Well, he wants an informal consultancy fee.'

'How much?' asked her mother.

'Ten thousand euros.'

There was a stunned silence.

'We don't have that sort of cash, Jacqueline,' gasped her mother.

'No more do any of us,' added Etienne, grimly.

'Then what are we going to do?' asked Jacqueline.

After another silence, she said coolly: 'We will ask this Mr Smith from England to lend us the money. And we will add it to the sum we will give him. Why not? It is the very least this Englishman can do. The English have always come here and appropriated everything. Their museums are full of their appropriation. He is going to get a very great deal for nothing. It is time for him to give us a gesture of good faith.'

That night, Etienne wrote another email.

From: etiennegrave@gouv.bj
To: johnsmith@btinternet.com

Dear Mr Smith, greetings again in the name of our Lord and Saviour Jesus Christ and thank you kindly for your email. The details of your bank account in Great Britain are gratefully received. However, most unexpectedly, we have a problem. We had hoped to get the funds into your account by the end of this working day. But the bank manager here in Cotonou has asked for an ex gratia payment of 10,000 euros to expedite this process discreetly and, as you can appreciate, this is technically irregular. We do not have the funds here. Time is of the essence. If this is not achieved very quickly then you might not receive the money at all. Please wire this sum via Western Union, via a cash pick-up at the Cotonou office. We can then add the sterling equivalent of this amount to your fee, which you will receive at the end of this week – in total, approximately 10,410,000 GB pounds. Please hurry, Mr Smith. There is no time to lose.

Kindly yours in Christ, E. Grave.

He added some wiring details as a postscript and pressed 'send'. Once again, Etienne, Jacqueline and Jacqueline's mother looked at each other gravely.

'I hope you know what you are doing, Etienne,' said Jacqueline's mother. 'How do we know we can trust this man?'

Etienne smiled placatingly. 'I am quite certain that everything will be all right, *maman*,' he replied – and instantly sensed that this endearment was unearned and profoundly misjudged. Jacqueline's mother stalked coldly off to bed.

Mr Smith's email arrived first thing the next morning and the household was so excited that Jacqueline's mother did not even react to Etienne's improper appearance at the breakfast table, brandishing Jacqueline's laptop.

From: johnsmith@btinternet.com
To: etiennegrave@gouv.bj

Dear Mr Grave, I was surprised to receive your email but I understand that these things have to be arranged quickly and quietly, and that occasionally squeaky wheels have to be greased. I am a man of the world. I have wired the sum of 10,000 euros to the cash pick-up point you specify. But please contact me later today to arrange the transfer.

Yours, John Smith.

Instantly, Jacqueline and her mother knew that Jacqueline's daily foot massage from Ode would have to be delayed while she picked up the money and took it to the bank. Her mother made a sharp inclination of the head as if to say: get on with it.

But it was three hours later, when Etienne and his future mother-in-law were seated at the kitchen table, discussing the relative merits of Richmond and Kew, that they heard the thin engine whine of Jacqueline's sleek little *moto*, and then Jacqueline herself entered, clearly deeply shaken. Without a word, she came in without taking off her shoes (a serious breach) and slumped down on the couch.

Her mother gave her a shrewd glance as if to ask: what is it?

Jacqueline took a swig from the Evian bottle in her bag and announced: 'I picked up the ten thousand euros from the Western Union office. It was all there. But when I gave it to the bank manager, he said he now wanted a hundred thousand euros.'

'In return for what?' gasped Etienne.

'In return for not telling anyone about the ten thousand euros.'

All three knew that it was futile to waste any more time and energy railing against the situation. With infinite weariness, Etienne slid Jacqueline's laptop towards him, closed the tab showing the website for Kew Gardens, and typed out another email.

From: etiennegrave@gouv.bj
To: johnsmith@btinternet.com

Dear Mr Smith, greetings in the name of Christ and the blessed Virgin. Thank you so much for your recent remittance. It is much appreciated. I must now ask you to remain calm and to summon all the energy and courage you have shown until now. We have hit another snag.

The technical irregularities of what you and I are doing, Mr Smith, have been noticed. The situation has become even more tense. I cannot rule out Interpol getting involved and you yourself finding the hot hand of your bobbies on your shoulder. Basically, another consultancy fee is required to make this happen and to keep it quiet. We need you to loan us the second sum of 100,000 euros.

Do not lose heart now, Mr Smith. If you do, everything we have done together, including the matter of your initial 10,000 euros, will have been for nothing. The net is closing in.

This is a once-in-a-lifetime opportunity. Please wire the 100,000 euros and the whole sum will be in your account in a few days.

Yours in the name of merciful God, E. Grave.

The next twelve hours were a torture. Etienne and Jacqueline checked the email inbox incessantly. There were calls from Madame Mende and various officials from the ministry and the police that Jacqueline's mother could use her recent grief to fend off. But this excuse couldn't last for ever. Finally, towards midnight, the email came through.

From: johnsmith@btinternet.com
To: etiennegrave@gouv.bj

Dear Mr Grave,

I must frankly say I was surprised and upset by your email. It really is a bit much. I assumed that you were on top of this situation. Do you appreciate what a position you have put me in with my wife, and indeed my brother-in-law, in whom I have also confided? I am very angry.

However, as you have given me your assurances, I have been able to get the support of family members with savings and I have today wired this second sum to the Western Union office in Cotonou. Please let me know immediately when you are ready to send me the whole sum.

Yours, John Smith

There was no need now for Jacqueline's mother to give her a meaningful nod. Jacqueline grabbed her bag and coat, rushed out of the door, and they heard the fierce mosquito whine of her manoeuvrable little *moto* as she headed off to the centre of the town, to pick up the new tranche of cash, make the required discreet payment and then come back, ready to transfer their own sum abroad.

For Jacqueline's mother and Etienne, the waiting was unbearable. They made no attempt to talk about Richmond, or Richmond Park, or Ham House and Garden. They just paced back and forth, like animals or caged lunatics, Etienne with his hands jammed into his pockets. Ode asked if they wanted tea and she was dismissed in the curtest possible way.

Finally, Jacqueline returned, flushed with excitement, her pupils almost entirely filling the irises, and announced: 'It is done. I got this man Smith's money and paid the manager. He has given me the transference codes' – she flourished a piece of paper – 'but we must act fast.'

Without another word, Etienne logged on to Jacqueline's late father's two accounts, and with barely a few keystrokes, transferred the equivalent of 130,000,000 pounds sterling into Mr Smith's account, and then sent him the following email:

From: etiennegrave@gouv.bj
To: johnsmith@btinternet.com

Dear Mr Smith, the transfer is now complete. You should see the entire sum in your account in the next hour. Will you now please get in touch, giving me your telephone number – a landline please, sir, if you would – so that we can make arrangements to transfer this sum onwards to another account, minus your commission and your 110,000 Euros?

Yours in Jesus, E. Grave

The hours went past and, worryingly, Mr Smith did not get back in touch. The composure of Jacqueline's mother, always fragile, disintegrated entirely. She called Etienne every name under the sun. Etienne endured these insults for a while, and then his own poise cracked and he began to shout back. The atmosphere was so awful that Jacqueline disappeared up to her room, hardly noticed by the other two. Etienne sent many more angry and desperate emails to Mr Smith, to no avail. And so this went on all night, without Jacqueline's mother or Etienne going to bed, or noticing Jacqueline's disappearance.

At the beginning of office hours the next morning, the phone rang, and Etienne, quite forgetting his place, snatched up the receiver. It was the bank manager.

'What do you want, you idiot? You scoundrel? Did we not give you your 110,000 euros?

'A hundred thousand? I specified the modest sum of ten thousand, M. Grave.'

It was at this moment that he noticed John Smith had replied to his email. He hung up the phone and read:

From: johnsmith@btinternet.com
To: etiennegrave@gouv.bj

Dear Mr Grave,

Thank you most kindly for the remittance, which I received in my bank account in good order. We should be in a position soon to transfer this sum into any UK account you specify. And if you can wait perhaps 24 or 48 hours, I think I have some good news for you. I have in fact, on the advice of my brother-in-law, taken the liberty of investing the entirety of this sum in a fund managed by Bernard L. Madoff Investment Securities LLC, and I am fully prepared to give you a share proportionate to your investment. I should be in a position to get back to you in two or perhaps three days.

Yours ever, John Smith

Etienne and Jacqueline's mother looked up from the computer and after Etienne said coldly: 'Where is Jacqueline?' They went together to her bedroom, and found no one there: an overnight bag had been packed, many of Jacqueline's clothes had gone. She had, however, left a Western Union receipt voucher for 100,000 euros on the immaculately folded counterpane.

NEIGHBOURS OF ZERO

People say life is a gamble, and by that, I mean people who've never gambled in their lives. People who don't know what they're talking about. Because life is not a gamble. Life is work. Doing stuff you mostly don't want to do, in return for money which will let you keep living, mostly to do stuff you don't want to do. All you're staking is time and energy, which you have to stake anyway, and which is running out anyway. Gambling is quite different. Trust me. I know what I'm talking about.

These days I like to go to the betting shops on a Friday or Saturday afternoon, after lunch, or possibly brunch. I like to have a sharpener before I go in. A livener. Basically it's the pre-betting shop aperitif or aperitives. It keeps me fresh. It keeps me loose. It keeps me where I need to be. Which is in the betting shop.

After provisionally bringing down the curtain on some strong lagers in the local Spoons I find myself in the bookmakers in Wood Green Shopping City, and it happens so quickly it's as if I've been teleported there or something. The atmosphere is amazingly welcoming. The other day the guy who works behind the counter did this sort of head-waiter 'your usual table sir?' gesture towards the roulette machines. I stand with all the other people playing but it's like urinals, you don't stand right next to them because that's inappropriate.

Classic roulette. Vegas roulette. Premier roulette. Lots of different roulettes. Basically the same. You put all your money into the machine to bet on even-money chances like red or black, odd or even, or you can make a bigger-odds bet, a single number at thirty-six to one. And it really is exciting the first time you win. First hit on the crack pipe. You can't believe it. You're up something like fifty or a hundred quid. All roulette players go through it: the one and only time you could cash out and walk away. But you never do. They should really have David Attenborough come along and point out the way these homo sapiens characters are hunched and tensed while they piss away their benefits and life-chances.

I love the way their bodies shiver and lurch when they win and the machine makes its *zzzznn* sound. But after a while, of course, they lose. They lose all their money. I stood next to someone last week who lost £720 in ten minutes. The guy walked away slowly like a chemo case in hospital, all he needed was pyjamas and a mobile IV. All over London you can see thousands and thousands of these machines sucking the money out of men.

It's like taking the red pill in *The Matrix*.

Now, here's the thing: I lose as well. Just a bit. Let me

explain. I'm with an outfit in Hornsey which has got quite a bit in cash through blaggings and weed sales and this cash has to be spruced up before it can be converted into the good things in life. No bank accepts deposits in cash, anyway. So I'm one of a number of people who take reasonably discreet sums, let's say a couple of hundred quid at a time, and park the cash, temporarily, in the fixed odds roulette betting terminal which swooshes it around for twenty minutes like a washing machine getting it Persil white.

I just stand there staring at the screen, occasionally knocking out a few one-pound bets. *Zzzzznnn. Zzzzznnn.* When I'm down to, say, £180 or £170, I conclude my session and go up to the main window and ask for the balance. And because it's a large sum of money, you can ask for a cheque. Totally legit. It's a completely reasonable request. People get robbed all the time in Wood Green Shopping City. Everyone knows you'll get your phone jacked in Burger King and you're very lucky if you can walk through Claire's Accessories without getting shot in the stomach. So I'm twenty or thirty quid down, but that's sort of like their commission, and some of the betting shop cashiers rumble you after a while, and they want their own little bit of iffy cash themselves. But that's the business, and nobody's complaining.

After a hard afternoon in the betting shop – I say afternoon; it's about twenty-five minutes – I'm away home to watch YouTube videos, maybe have a bath and a bit of a relax. Then it's back to Spoons to break bread with my associate and employer, Mr Lemuel 'The Lemster' Pumphrey and his lady common-law wife Jean, in whose joint names I have asked the bookies to make out the cheque. There is the handover, and at the same time Lem gives me some clean banknotes by way of payment. I am, however, expected to get them some drinks out of this. It's another commission, and again there are no complaints. Certainly not from me.

But anyway. This all changed when a strange thing started happening. The Lemster was on brusque form on the phone just after breakfast one day, entrusting me with a large cash sum, which he had apparently got from a recent big job. Said he needed it through the system pretty quick and didn't mind if the betting shop took a bigger commission than usual. His deadpan associate called round with it after an hour or so and I went straight to Wood Green without stopping for a livener. And the moment I arrived at the bookies I knew something was wrong.

There was a disturbance in the force.

One of the glass panes outside was cracked.

The cashier had a black eye.

But I just carried on. Just took my place next to all the losers and started playing. And that's when I noticed this betting option that I didn't know about before. It's called Neighbours of Zero. It's a nine-chip bet on the clutch of seventeen numbers either side of zero on the roulette wheel, from 22 black round to 25 red. If one of the numbers comes up, you win at 2 to 1. You might as well put it on red or black, mightn't you?

But I had a good feeling. A weird good feeling. I put down a Neighbours of Zero. Four black. *Zzzzznn.* I win. Twenty quid. I did another, upping the punt. Eighteen red. *Zzzzznn.* I win. Hundred quid. Cranked up the punt again for my third one. Zero. *Zzzzznn.* I win. Five hundred quid. House maximum payout.

I was floating. I was buzzing. I had the touch. I had the groove. I did a string of Neighbours of Zero bets. Got up to nine thousand pounds. Nobody was noticing. But I knew that if things went on like this, the cashier was going to clock the problem, and in cases like this he's on a promise from HQ to pull the plug on some pretext. It was a miracle he hadn't intervened before. I cashed out. Got a separate big cheque for myself and the usual smaller one for Lemster.

I just couldn't help myself in the pub that evening. Drinks all round for Mr and Mrs Pumphrey and their various granite-faced associates, and I even got a bit merry myself. Where did the original capital come from, I made so bold as to ask. Job in Wood Green Shopping City, said Lem – bookies.

Jesus. Of course, the broken glass, the cashier's black eye. I was betting the betting shop's stolen money. I had created a vortex in the money continuum. It was like typing 'Google' into Google. It created a karmic black hole. The universe was haemorrhaging money through the conceptual anus of existence into my bank account. That's why I kept winning. The cosmic order of things was turned in on itself. I could never lose. This was exciting.

The next day I won £37,000 on a series of Neighbours of Zero bets, just after the shop opened at eight in the morning. Enough for a lovely deposit on a buy-to-let.

But the next day, my winning streak was over. I walked in to find that the roulette machine had gone. The money tree had been chopped down. And in its place a pompous little sign from the management declaring that they had decided to withdraw Fixed Odds Betting Terminals because they were encouraging people to gamble irresponsibly. I was stunned. Cunts.

And that was when there was a God-almighty crash and a couple of tricky customers come barging in with a shooter and said, in voices I recognised from my soirées with Lemmy, that everybody should get down because this was a robbery.

The silly sods had only decided to hit the place a second time, just as I was there; that was all.

I was actually the only one there and I'd ducked down behind one of the central standing-level islands that people use to make bets, writing with the little free pens. They hadn't seen me. Of course, the cashier hands over whatever he's got in the till, good as gold. One of the guys puts this in an Adidas bag, and actually puts it down near the door while he checks his phone. It's a robbery and this guy's actually checking his Facebook. Two thumbs of course. Meanwhile his mate threatens the poor sod a bit more. It was at that point that I sneezed in my hiding place – actually sneezed.

'Who the fuck is that?'

I stayed hiding. There was no point trying to convince them that we were all on the same team. They probably didn't even know about me and what I was doing for the Lemster. They just thought I was a punter, taking the piss.

The bookies actually had a wide shopfront: two doors. From where I was hiding, I could see them both — one was fringed in black and one in red, in honour of the roulette theme, of course. This guy was advancing on where I was crouching and I had just a few seconds to bet on which door to make a run for. If I got the unguarded one, I was out of there and in the clear. But if I got it wrong, I'd bump straight into the other bloke's arms and his colleague would clump me pretty hard. I'd probably get brain damage.

Red or black? Red or black?

I went for black.

It came up.

Doorway completely clear, and I scooped up their Adidas

bag on the way out, ran down the walkway, and ducked down the staff-only stairwell just by Foot Locker that I sometimes use to urinate when I'm a bit lairy and can't be bothered to make it to the toilet. I heard the alarm go off behind me. Some instinct told me to stop running, start behaving like a respectable member of the public which is what I was. I came back out to find two special constables had actually apprehended the villains, along with two security guards and a have-a-go member of the public. That gun was a toy. It was only when I got home that I thought to look in the bag: nine hundred and fifty quid. Not bad.

As I say: that's gambling for you. I'm not interested anyway. Now what I want to know is – how do you get to open a betting shop? With a roulette machine? That's my business now.

MY PLEASURE

Frank Glover was proud of his body – prouder than he had ever been as a young man. And in his teens and twenties, there really had been something to be proud of. Frank loved sports at school. At university in the seventies he had even boxed, winning by an actual knockout one evening at the Cambridge Guildhall, that bleary and gritty venue which, the evening before, had played host to a sellout performance by The Bootleg Beatles. Those were the days. Frank could eat whatever he wanted without ever putting on weight, and he was always hungry. But he was never vain. There were no extant photographs of him as an adult in a swimming costume. In that pre-Instagram era, photographs were themselves a rarity.

In his late thirties, as a result of a sedentary and hard-drinking career in sports journalism, Frank started to put on weight. And he made a concerted decision to correct that. He took up running, counted calories, cut back on drink and cut out cheese entirely. His body never again attained that easy, effortless lankiness of youth. But now there was a willed sleekness to the way he looked that pleased him. A consciously earned triumph.

Frank had been divorced twice; he was on reasonable terms with both ex-wives, but had a prickly relationship with the grown-up daughter from his first marriage, Rowena Glover, who was now the author of bestselling romantic fiction. Frank himself worked for an evening newspaper in London, covering events in his own genially incurious style – unchanged over decades. Big events in football, cricket, Formula One – you name it. He also had his own humorous weekly column, though he noticed that whenever he took a week off, his replacement was a sharp and industrious young woman on the staff who took a far more satirical and subversive attitude to sport's various organisational bodies and achieved her comic effects more quickly, more powerfully and even more knowledgeably.

Frank was on the verge of retirement. He knew that. At sixty, he was in a position to cash in a uniquely generous pension. He had actually been called in for a chat with the managing editor to discuss precisely this, and had been told he might even continue with his column on a freelance basis.

So he wasn't unhappy with the way his career was ending up, especially as something rather agreeable had just happened to him. He had been invited as a regular guest on a national TV breakfast programme, reviewing the morning newspapers and, without any experience at all, he proved to be an absolute natural. He found exactly the right banteringly flirtatious tone with the female presenter. Frank had become a minor celebrity.

It was in this pleasantly invigorating state that he met Louise Bartley, a very attractive young woman who had just been hired as executive assistant to the arts and literary editor, Natasha Howe. Louise had laughed obligingly and intuitively at the self-deprecatory remark Frank had made when Natasha introduced Frank to her as the 'biggest star on the paper'. She positively beamed when Natasha, on a whim, suggested the three of them pop out to the café around the corner from the newspaper building for lunch.

Frank pulled out Louise's chair for her; she thanked him with an intriguing demureness, and he replied with some anodyne remark, a remark he could hardly hear himself making above the sound of his blood thumping in his ears. Frank found Louise devastatingly attractive. She was flirting with him – wasn't she? That moment when the back of her hand brushed against his, that was deliberate – wasn't it?

Natasha, Frank and Louise had a highly cordial lunch at which they shared a single bottle of wine, a rare indulgence for the modern newspaper industry. They ambled back to the office at half past two.

'Well, that was very nice!' said Louise. 'It was lovely to meet you!'

'We must do it again soon!' said Frank breezily.

'Ooh, yes please!' said Louise.

Frank returned to his desk, simmering with erotic surmise.

He didn't think of himself as a womaniser. There was something tacky and nasty about that. He despised the idea. He thought of himself as reasonably enlightened. Both of his marriages had ended because of his infidelities, which he argued were merely symptoms of a deeper malaise. But it was a malaise that he did not care to investigate any further than the point at which it theoretically cleared him personally of blame.

He saw Louise around the office and they flashed each other dazzling smiles. One Monday morning he received this email from her:

From: lbartley32@gmail.com
To: fglover@londoncourier.co.uk
February 2, 2019
I thought you did very well on the telly on Saturday!

Frank decided that this was his moment.

From: fglover@londoncourier.co.uk
To: lbartley32@gmail.com
February 2, 2019
Very sweet of you. Would you like to have lunch on Friday at that Italian place in Warwick Street that's been getting those great reviews?

(Here he actually linked to the restaurant's website.)

From: lbartley32@gmail.com
To: fglover@londoncourier.co.uk
February 2, 2019
Great!

Frank waited five minutes and then sent another email:

From: fglover@londoncourier.co.uk

To: lbartley32@gmail.com
February 2, 2019
Darn it! They're booked solid for lunch that day, but they can do dinner at 7:30. How would that be?

If Louise had said a cautious no to this, or even wondered politely about other days for lunch, Frank was prepared to rein in his fantasies, be realistic, and forget the whole thing. But she replied immediately:

From: lbartley32@gmail.com
To: fglover@londoncourier.co.uk
February 2, 2019
Wonderful! See you then! x

Frank spent the next few days in an almost hysterical state of anticipation. He was about to have dinner *à deux* with a beautiful woman who seemed attracted to him. His saliva tasted almost metallic with lust. Could he be on the verge of a new relationship? Did he have one left in him? He was sixty years old. It was the age at which both his father and elder brother had died. But Frank didn't feel old. At sixty, he felt the way he had felt in his late forties – which at the time felt to him not so different from his mid-thirties.

The day before the dinner, Frank made a momentous decision. He visited, in person, a fashionable boutique hotel that was next door to the restaurant – and made a provisional booking for the night of his dinner. The reason for this was that his own flat was an unsexy overground rail journey away. He wanted to impress, to astonish Louise with his brazen hotel suggestion, at the end of a sexually charged evening. He wanted to reach across the table to take her hand. He wanted to murmur to her that they could repair to the hotel across the road.

From: lbartley32@gmail.com
To: fglover@londoncourier.co.uk
February 5, 2019
Looking forward to our dinner! Lx

Frank was almost faint with excitement.

The date of their rendezvous dawned, and Frank consciously avoided seeing Louise at the office all that day, not wanting to tarnish the specialness of that evening's planned encounter. He was at the restaurant at seven, fully thirty minutes in advance, asked for a glass of wine, and went into a reverie. What would it be like when they went to the hotel together? Would she want Frank to turn all the lights off before they went to bed? Would they gently undress each other? What would it be like?

Frank took another gulp of wine. Would Louise gasp or murmur his name when they were in bed? Would she fall in love with him? Was Frank in love with her now?

'Frank!'

Frank looked up, and there Louise was, voluptuous in a gorgeous pale dress cinched at the waist with a thin leather belt. Her shoulder-length blonde hair seemed to glimmer with highlights. She smiled dazzlingly.

Louise! Please, sit down.'

She placed her bag on the third seat at the table and sat.

'Should I get a bottle?'

'Oh, well, just a glass!'

Louise smiled brilliantly again and Frank felt his heart

melt. They ordered, drank, and over the first course, Frank was electrified as Louise leant over and said: 'Frank, I've got something to tell you.'

'What?'

'I'm pregnant!'

Louise had been looking forward all day to telling her lovely new friend Frank that she was going to start a family with her partner Ben, who worked in IT for an online poker site, but in fact earned less than her. Frank had such a nice face, and he reminded her an awful lot of her dad, who had died of cancer the year before. On the Tube on the way to the restaurant, Louise had almost cried thinking of the resemblance, and thinking of the fact that her dad would never hear about the fact that she was going to have a baby, died before getting to be a granddad. Telling Frank was the next best thing, a poignant idea that nearly made her burst into tears all over again.

At twenty-nine, Louise was really nervous about being a mum, really nervous also about asking her new employer for maternity leave almost immediately after being hired. She also hoped that Frank might help with this, being such a senior figure in the organisation. A television star as well!

Frank seemed very surprised when she told him the news, and that was understandable. She could see that it was surprising that she should confide something so important to him, someone who was almost a complete stranger. But he was no nice. And she was bursting with the news. It was the most wonderful thing that had ever happened to her. And in her secret heart, Louise had been a little disappointed with Ben's own rather muted reaction. He had hugged her, but then almost instantly started worrying about money.

Louise noticed how Frank had for a microsecond also

seemed unsure how to react. But then he smiled really nicely and said congratulations. They had a lovely chat about families and he had talked about bringing up his own daughter, who of course had grown up long ago. He had changed nappies: a modern man! Looking back on the dinner, though, Louise wondered if had seemed a little bit subdued. There was a strange sadness in his eyes that she hadn't noticed before. An awful thought struck her after the dinner, when she was on her way home on the train.

Did Frank disapprove of the fact that she and Ben were not married?

She knew that her mum felt that way, and she was almost sure she noticed Frank's glance flicking to her left hand to confirm the lack of a ring. There was a sadness in his eyes, she thought, and it reminded her of a strange sadness that she sometimes saw in her dad's eyes when she was growing up, when he would gaze out of the window in the morning when the family were having breakfast. Perhaps she and Ben could get married, but there was no time to organise that before her due date. Louise felt unhappy and frustrated. When was someone going to react with the joy that she felt?

She walked from the Tube station and let herself into the flat she shared with Ben in Barnet; after getting through the front door, it meant negotiating her way past the three bikes that her neighbours had inconsiderately left in the hallway, and all the pizza-delivery and minicab leaflets that no one but her ever cleared up and put on the little low table next to the doormat. She climbed up the two flights of stairs – already she could see how this was tiring her out – reached the flat door, effortlessly opened that, put her keys in a little saucer on the shelf by the door and turned on the lights.

Ben wasn't home yet.

She looked at the front room, with its single couch and an armchair angled to face the big widescreen TV, almost as big as the couch, in fact. She found herself looking at all the pictures of her and Ben that were dotted about the room, as if to check they were all still there. Photographs of them on holiday in Italy, in Greece, in America – New York! As ever, Louise noticed that Ben's face and smile were so identical every time that the same image could have been photoshopped into each shot. They had lived in this flat together for five years, and what's more they had bought it. They shared the mortgage. In a way, they already were married.

Ben wasn't the first man she had ever slept with. He was the sixth, although she had told him he was the third. The others she secretly decided were irrelevant; inadmissible: two one-night stands at university, and a brief and deeply horrible liaison with her married lecturer, who curtly informed her the relationship was at an end over coffee at a place well away from campus, then added that if necessary he would deny everything and walked out of the café without actually saying goodbye. She had met Ben in her final year.

Louise checked the time. It was half past nine. Unusual for Ben not to be home. She WhatsApped him. No reply.

After putting the kettle on and making herself a peppermint tea, she did the thing she looked forward to most during the day. Cradling the cup in her palms, she walked into the second bedroom which she and Ben had repurposed as a 'nursery'. They didn't know the baby's sex yet, and were in any case unsure whether to do anything as obvious as decorate it in blue or pink, so they had instead chosen a warm sunlit canary-yellow, with a decorative band around the walls bearing a recurrent motif – a succession of cantering ponies encircling the room. There, by the window, looking down on the garden belonging to the ground-floor flat, was the waist-high changing table, next to it the large and cumbersome buggy, as incongruous as keeping a family car indoors. Both of these were presents from Ben's parents. In the middle of the floor was the cot. Louise would often wonderingly reach down into it, pressing her fingertips into the shallow mattress, covered with its white nylon fitted sheet.

That is where the baby would be. It would be into this cot that she would lower the baby when he or she was asleep, and from which she or Ben would lift the baby when he or she cried in the middle of night. Now the cot was dramatically vast and tensely empty, like a football stadium an hour before the match. The mystery of the future exalted Louise. She didn't know if she felt happy or sad.

The baby. When the baby comes. The nurse at the health centre loved to cut out the definite article: baby, when baby comes, and so on, as if 'baby' was the name or nickname of someone already familiar, and Louise knew that was supposed to reassure her, and maybe that was the effect it had on all the other mums-to-be, but not on her. It was weird and a bit creepy and she didn't have time to get married before the baby came and she felt her mind starting to get into a dizzying rush or crush, just like when she was little and couldn't get to sleep and found herself thinking about her name: Louise, Louise, Louise.

She placed the palms of her hands over her eye sockets, took them away, looked down, saw the cup down on the floor, on its side, the tea having made an ugly splash-stain on the new carpet, and suddenly Ben was there beside her, having not even taken his coat off, holding her in his arms.

'Oh, Loulou, what's the matter?' he said with an air of gentle dismay, signalling that he already broadly knew what the matter was.

Louise carried on sobbing into his shoulder.

'Please Lou, don't worry, you mustn't worry.'

She sobbed.

'What's the matter?'

'Ben, I'm so scared. I'm so scared.'

'Why?'

'It's…I'm not ready. I'm not ready.'

'Loulou, it is scary. I'm scared too. But we'll be ready for it together. I promise. OK?'

Louise nodded and smiled.

'I love you.'

'I love you, too.'

CAREER MOVE

Hollywood would always be his first love, but Satan also adored the London West End stage and, like all intelligent theatregoers, deplored the current prevalence of musicals and the paucity of new writing. In fact, he made a point of attending first nights of original plays. He would often wait discreetly in the bar until a few moments before curtain-up (scheduled half an hour earlier than usual, of course, to give the newspaper critics time to write their reviews) hoping to catch a glimpse of the author himself, sneaking about, chatting nervously to supportive friends and acquaintances, anxiously scanning the auditorium to see who was 'in front' – and oh, how Satan loved those quaint theatrical terms!

This is where he was to be seen now, at a London theatre for a premiere, dressed in a comfortably fitting dark jacket and pale chinos, his thick, grey-black hair swept straight back from his forehead, spectacles looped casually into an open shirt-front. He looked like a visiting Canadian academic, and as the house lights dimmed, it was an air of quiet authority and purpose which allowed him to rise from his aisle seat in the stalls, walk out into the corridor and through a door marked 'private' (actually holding the door open for a bona fide member of staff who smiled and said thank you) and from there into the wings, in whose shadows he was able to observe the play's author closely. Satan savoured this man's desperate need for success as he tensely watched the action from the side of the stage, silently mouthing every syllable of his dialogue as it was being performed.

The author's name was Anthony Marcus, a talented dramatist with a number of works commissioned by the National Theatre – though the last of these was fully a decade previously. There were also some television credits and an unproduced movie screenplay. He was in his late thirties, married with three children. This current play, now getting its West End transfer after a moderately successful appearance at Chichester, was entitled *Caring*, and concerned a thirtyish married woman who has an affair with the family's Croatian male nanny. A well-known television actress played the lead; the role of the nanny, or 'manny' as he was whimsically described, was taken by a young comedian, who had become famous through appearances on a television panel game. The play had been notable for the fully nude sex scene just before the interval, which had been getting a gratifying combination of laughs and gasps, and so it proved again that evening.

When the final curtain came down, there was much applause and whooping from a packed house: the PR had taken care to give away tickets to make sure every seat was taken.

Satan stepped quickly out of the wings into the corridor that led to Dressing Rooms One and Two, and by darting up a tiny flight of cramped steps that led round to a fire escape, he was able to scramble quickly down into the small car park area outside the stage door and then, after a twenty-minute wait, follow the cast, the director and Anthony himself at a discreet distance as they headed for a little Italian restaurant where a table and back room had been reserved for them.

Satan took a table for one on his own, ordering a plate of linguine and a glass of Rioja and, by craning his neck occasionally, was able to keep the raucous theatrical party under surveillance.

Things went on like this for an hour and a half; it was nearing midnight, and Satan noticed that the table's first-night mood was perceptibly beginning to sour, with the cast periodically checking their phones, frowning, shrugging and putting them away again. The one person not doing this, Satan noticed, was Anthony, deep into animated conversation with the director.

Satan checked his own phone and saw for himself the news that was extinguishing the euphoria. All the national newspaper reviews were now online and they were universally bad. One-star pans and two-star shrugs. The acting, direction and especially the script roundly attacked. Only Anthony, it seemed, hadn't yet noticed.

Then Stephen O'Riordan, the producer who had brought the show into London, came into the restaurant with his associate Kay Bruscha. Both their faces were set into a patently insincere professional smile, and they did not take the two places which had been reserved for them at the table.

'Hello everyone. Well done!' Stephen called out to the group, who bravely raised their glasses to him. Anthony jumped up and went over.

'Stephen!' he cried. 'You were right! You were right! You were right! Of course it was going to go over with London audiences. Of course it was. What was I thinking? Will you have a drink?'

'Can we have a chat outside, Anthony?' asked Kay.

'Of course.' Satan watched Anthony's face fall and intuited that he was at this moment realising that he hadn't checked the reviews. The grim trio left the restaurant for a conversation in the street, and Satan followed, on the pretext that he was trying to get a better signal on his phone, making a show of holding it up around him at arm's length at various angles.

'Anthony, look,' said Stephen heavily, holding out to him a summary of the reviews on his iPad. 'The advance sales are very poor and these reviews are damaging. I might as well tell you sooner rather than later. We're going to have to close the show. I'm sorry to tell you this now, but there is no point avoiding it. You knew this was a real long shot. We won't make any announcement yet, but we're closing the run on Saturday week. I'm very sorry, Anthony. But this is it.'

Swallowing his shock, Anthony said goodbye to them, and then after staring sightlessly ahead of him for about half a minute, shook his head a little and went back into the restaurant. Explaining to the now subdued party that Kay and Stephen had had to go, but that they wanted to congratulate everyone on a great opening night, Anthony said that he had to leave himself. He congratulated Dave Collins, the comic playing the nanny. Then he turned to Melissa Entwistle, the beautiful actress playing the lead, and tilting his head to one side went in for a hug, to which Melissa consented, though clearly she had no great liking for Anthony – something that continued to depress him. The distance, brevity and hint of distaste in her hug triggered a resurgence in his despair, and Anthony knew that he was going to have to leave now. Anthony drove home, tiptoed into the bedroom where his wife was still awake, told her the news and burst into tears.

News of the closure got out almost immediately. He received friendly, sympathetic emails from fellow writers, in each and every case enjoying greater success. His wife Beth was gentle and supportive, but it seemed to them both that with no money coming in from his writing it could be her income, from a job in publishing, that they might have to rely on for the time being, and that his career might in fact have peaked.

Anthony became deeply depressed.

He saw Beth off in the morning, took the children to school, and then, instead of beginning work, he would watch daytime television or just go back to bed, although he never neglected to pick the children up from school again, or have something ready for Beth when she got home. He was careful always to keep his depression as invisible as possible.

There was only one thing which got Anthony out of the house – one activity which he regularly undertook, with a mixture of pleasure and resentful melancholy – and that was going to the gym. Private gym membership was something he had bought when *Caring* had looked as if it was going to be a hit. He had seven months left to run on his card, and was now grimly determined to make the most of it.

He enjoyed the running machines, in front of which the management had positioned amusing virtual-reality screens, which showed a scrolling forward-perspective image of a sun-dappled woodland glade through which the exerciser could imagine himself to be running. Anthony usually found himself alone on these machines, but would lately have the curious sense that someone was exercising on the one to his left. He would glance around; there was no one there. Then one morning, as he was puffing and lumbering, a cool male voice said: 'Tough luck about the play.'

He stopped and turned to see a man in early middle age on the belt next to his, in a light grey sweatshirt, with grey-black hair swept straight back from his forehead; he had the casually dynamic look of a billionaire software designer.

'Thanks,' said Anthony, with a rueful, embarrassed smile, uncomfortable at having to discuss a painful subject with a complete stranger.

'I was there on opening night. It was great. I'm such an admirer of your work: I loved *The Ballad of Charles Taylor*, *Fuzzy Logic* and *Comrades*.'

'Wow,' smiled Anthony, relaxing a little. 'You are a fan. That last one only went on at the Hampstead Theatre.'

'Oh yes,' continued the man, with a mild earnestness. 'And I adored your episode of *Inspector Havisham*: the one about the circus dwarf getting killed on the trapeze.'

'Christ! That was in the early nineties.'

'But my favourite has to be that play about the two brothers locked inside the room and you're not sure if there's been a nuclear holocaust outside, or if they've just had some sort of joint mental breakdown.'

This last was a piece which Anthony had written for his school drama class when he was fifteen.

'Who are you?' he said in a quiet voice.

'Satan,' the man replied, easily. 'And I think I can help you with your career.'

In the weeks and months that were to follow, Anthony told himself that his subsequent behaviour in this man's company was entirely consistent with that of someone attempting to humour a crazy person, and that this must therefore have been what was happening.

'What do you mean? Will you please go away?'

'I mean that I can give you the highest possible success in your career,' smiled Satan, 'but that I shall require something in return. As to going away: yes of course, if you wish it.'

Satan did not move.

'Just, just go away.'

Satan remained still, and then smiled, as if at some absurd evasion, or prevarication.

'I'll tell you what I'm going to do. I'm going to give you a free sample. A gift. No obligation. No strings. You can just have it.'

Frowning, pale, Anthony turned away and stared at the 'glade' screen.

'Your lead actress, Melissa Entwhistle. Do you want to have sex with her?'

'Will you please go away?' snapped Anthony.

'You know,' said Satan mildly, 'I didn't ask if it was right to have sex with her. I just asked do you want to.'

'Whoever you are, you're being crass, stupid and offensive. Kindly go away!'

Satan gave it a moment, and then twirled away with a smile, made to leave, and just at the door, turned around and grinningly pointed his forefinger at Anthony like a cocked pistol. 'You have fun now!' And he went.

The last night 'wake' for Anthony's failed play was to take

place in Dave Collins' flat in Camden Town: Anthony's wife had taken the children away to her parents for the weekend, so Anthony was alone. After some thought, he decided to go to the final performance of *Caring* – however painful that would be – and then come on to Dave's party, carrying a sheepish bottle of wine.

Once there, he was surprised and gratified to find himself the centre of attention; his arrival was greeted with supportive, sympathetic and celebratory acclaim. He had not made his presence known to the cast at the theatre, so turning up at Dave's door was a big and evidently wonderful surprise. Coming into the living room got a cheer from the cast, who seemed to feel for him, and adore him. And the most extraordinarily warm reception came from Melissa Entwhistle herself.

Throughout the run, Melissa had very been cool to Anthony, and he was humbly in awe of her gorgeous, glamorous unattainability: a quality that he, a happily married man, in any case assessed only in the most theoretical way. She was a star who appeared in gossip magazines and tabloids almost every day in the company of A-list film actors, DJs and supermodels. Anthony had often tried to strike up conversations with Melissa when he turned up to rehearsals, and been all but blanked. Her polite gaze habitually slid away from his, and Anthony discovered just how low the author was on the prestige ladder. Yet now things were different.

'Anthony! Anthony!' Melissa came up to him, snaked two arms around his neck and kissed him, lingeringly, on the lips. 'Come and get a drink,' she breathed at last. If Anthony had been Melissa's actual boyfriend, she could not have been more casually tactile with him. She had her arm through his, or actually around his waist, from then on, continually giggling and whispering and mussing his hair. Anthony, amazed, tried to behave in such a way as to suggest that all this was the result of some pre-existing private joke. Glances were exchanged and eyes widened behind his back, and they were exchanged and widened yet more at the end of the evening, when Melissa said she was in no condition to drive – and could Anthony take her home? Her friends and acquaintances had seen her drinking many times, but this was an incredible change of attitude.

Anthony, who had not been drinking much at all, drove to Melissa's flat in South Kensington. They parked just outside, and Melissa leaned over and kissed him again, lingeringly.

'Come up for a coffee,' she whispered. So Anthony went up for a coffee.

He had never been unfaithful to his wife in ten years of marriage, but tripped up the stairs behind Melissa in an erotic daze of unbelieving excitement.

Once inside, Melissa turned on a switch which appeared to activate low, romantic lighting throughout the apartment. She threw her coat onto the couch and turned to Anthony. 'So – would you like coffee? Or should we just take our clothes off and pop straight into bed?'

This is in fact what happened. The resulting activity was concluded satisfactorily enough from Anthony's point of view, but he was unsure how to behave afterwards. Throughout long years of monogamous partnership, he had occasionally wondered what infidelity would feel like, but had never predicted this blankness, this otherness. Like a Lottery winner, he could only imagine that it had not yet sunk in. With a dreamy, sated smile Melissa looked like drifting off to sleep, and Anthony was just wondering if he might actually permit himself to do the same thing, right next to her, when something very strange happened.

'Hey!' she said sharply, awakening him from a light doze. Anthony could not tell exactly how much time had elapsed. He opened his eyes and was startled by what he saw. Melissa was now sitting up in bed, pale, staring straight ahead. Her face seemed thinner, starker. Her languorous manner had quite disappeared, and she now looked shocked, as if by the appearance of a ghost. Anthony reached up to caress her, and she brushed his hand away, with a shiver of disgust.

'You – you need to go now,' she said, in a wondering, horrified voice.

'OK,' said Anthony, softly and warily. "Can I…can I call you tomorrow?'

Melissa simply shook her head, still staring straight ahead.

'You need to go. Go now. Go.'

Anthony now sat up and looked her intently.

'Are you OK?'

Melissa turned to look at him, and instantly turned away, with the same expression of shock. She looked very ill.

'Just go.'

After this, Anthony found it difficult to concentrate, and Beth sadly attributed this to all the same feelings of depression and frustration. He made no headway with his new screenplay. The A4 page blinked at him from his computer screen in all its pure, virginal whiteness. He took the kids to school and brought them back. He went for walks. He did the occasional book review. He checked his phone frequently for messages: nothing. He called Melissa once, and got her voicemail – not her voicemail actually, but the generic Vodaphone message. He hung up. Anthony wondered when the feelings of shame and guilt would set in, but found that they were present only in the mildest and most theoretical form – chiefly at the realisation that he did not, in fact, have these feelings. He felt mainly a sort of numb fearfulness: a fear of thinking what that fateful evening meant.

Many times, he walked past the gym, and could clearly see the two running machines, side by side, through the window. Would he have another encounter there? After a week, the inevitable could be delayed no longer. Anthony airily announced to Beth one morning that he fancied 'a little workout' and walked in a stiff-legged trot to the fitness centre, trying not to break into a run.

After a jittery change into his workout clothes, he went round to the running machines, and found who he was looking for, spryly jogging on the left-hand belt. Anthony self-consciously took his own position and coyly attempted to begin a conversation.

'Hi!' he said.

'Hello,' said Satan coolly, blankly, and looked away, continuing to run. Clearly it was up to Anthony to swallow his pride and show a little more humility with his new friend.

'I, um, I just wanted to say…'

'Yes?'

'I wanted to say thank you for the nice things you said about my plays. I actually looked up some of my, um, biographical newspaper profiles online, and I guess those articles were where you found out about my school play. I'm sure you weren't at my school. Ha!'

Anthony gave a nervous little laugh, as if joshingly congratulating Satan on his mischievous ingenuity. He had actually found absolutely no reference to this boyhood work in any of the journalistic profiles or interviews. But it was important to Anthony to construct some sort of face-saving, sanity-saving explanation for his friend's knowledge, and indeed their continuing acquaintance.

Satan stopped running and turned to look at Anthony.

'I see,' he said pointedly, with a thin smile. 'And that was why you wanted to thank me, was it?'

Anthony blushed, and looked down.

'How is Beth, incidentally?'

Anthony looked up, startled, and Satan raised an emollient palm. 'Those newspaper profiles – remember? They mentioned her name. Didn't they?'

Anthony supposed that they did. Both relaxed a little, and ran in silence. After a minute, Anthony plucked up the courage to ask, in the same strained, bantering tone: 'So, hah, how long have you been having a laugh, introducing yourself to total strangers, as, um, as…' Anthony faltered at the last moment.

Satan met his gaze levelly. 'Sometimes I introduce myself and sometimes not. I introduced myself to you because I admire your work.'

Humbly, Anthony nodded several times, swallowed and looked down.

'So. Have you thought any more about what I said?'

'You mean – about my career?'

'Yes. Your career. What do you want?'

Again, Anthony attempted to make light of this question.

'What do I want? Well, hah, I don't know. Who knows?'

'Of course you know. Everybody knows. Some people don't like to admit it to themselves, in case they don't get it. Only idiots fail to imagine their own futures.'

'Well, I, um…'

'Let me ask you a question,' interrupted Satan sharply. 'I'm going to ask you a simple question – not a personal one, not an embarrassing one – just a very, very easy one. And you must answer honestly. All right?'

'All right.'

'Which tastes nicer: chocolate or fresh fruit?'

'Well,' said Anthony. 'You can't really…'

'Shut up,' snapped Satan, and his sudden contempt was like a riding crop across Anthony's face. 'Listen, you nincompoop. I didn't ask you if fruit tastes nice, and I didn't ask if it was healthier than chocolate. I asked which tastes nicer, and what is the obvious answer?'

Anthony hung his head, like a naughty schoolboy. 'Chocolate,' he mumbled. 'Chocolate tastes nicer.'

Satan relaxed and patted his pupil on the arm. 'Yes. Of course. But why can't we admit it straight away? What absurd piety makes us flinch from the truth?'

There was silence for a moment.

'So,' Satan resumed. 'What do you want?'

Again, Anthony attempted an air of helpless bemusement at the question.

'Well… Wealth isn't everything of course. Is it? I mean… very poor people are happy. Aren't they?'

'Oh yes. And some homeless tramps have a great head of hair. It's a question of priorities. But in any case, I don't think being rich is exactly what you want, is it?'

There was a pause and finally Anthony spoke.

'I suppose I want what everyone wants: success. I want my plays and film-scripts to be produced, and I want them to be a success, a big success.'

'You suppose. You suppose you want this.'

'All right, no, there's no "suppose" about it. I do want this.'

'And what do you imagine? What do you fantasise about? The ultimate moment of success, what is it?'

'Erm, I...' Anthony laughed, feebly. 'Winning the Nobel Prize for Literature?'

Satan's eyes became veiled with scepticism and derision. 'Ah yes. The Nobel Prize. Wearing white tie in some distant, blond-wood hall in Sweden – or is it Norway? Shaking hands with the king, in that dull untelevised ceremony. That's truly what you fantasise about it, is it?'

'No. No, it isn't.'

Again, there was silence, and Satan smiled shrewdly. He said: 'I think I can guess what you dream about.'

Anthony looked up at him, and his feeling of fear, never far away, suddenly surged again as Satan's smiling face loomed up to his.

'Do you want to win an Academy Award?'

Anthony said nothing.

'An Oscar – for best screenplay? An impossibly elegant, witty speech? Swathed in glamour and triumph on both sides of the Atlantic?'

Eventually, Anthony nodded and even smiled, pressing his lips ruefully together. 'Yes. Yes that is what I'd like.'

'What you'd like? Or what you want?'

'What I want. What I want.'

Satan laughed.

'Well you can have it. No problem. Nothing's easier. You can have the Oscar in a few years' time. But I want something in return. Not I'd like. I want.'

At this moment, Anthony attempted some derision of his own.

'Yeah, right. You want my immortal soul.'

'No, no. Nothing so important.'

'Then…then, what do you want?'

'On a certain date, which we will agree between us, I want to hit your youngest child.'

Anthony's next question, into which he tried to inject utter bafflement, was: 'How hard?'

'This hard,' said Satan and, with shocking force, struck Anthony across the face with his open hand. It was like being hit by the fixed wing-mirror of a speeding truck. Anthony was lifted off his feet, flew backwards and crashed against the wall. After a few seconds, the music being piped over the PA gulped out and the gym attendant rushed in to see what on earth had happened. Satan was already standing over him, helping him up.

'It's nothing,' he said over his shoulder to the doubtful, sweatshirted gym employee. 'My friend just slipped over. He's fine. Aren't you?'

'I'm fine,' said Anthony in a tiny voice. Something compelled him to keep the assault a secret.

'Fuck!' he squeaked when the attendant had gone. 'You fucking maniac. What the fuck was that?'

'That? That was nothing,' shrugged Satan. 'It hurt at the time, but now it's over, isn't it? It's all over. You're big enough to shrug it off, aren't you? No bones broken. It was nothing.'

Anthony breathed heavily, staring hard at Satan's calm, smiling face, and then looked away. He had to admit it: Satan was right. Being hit like that was painful and humiliating, but even as they spoke, he could see how the shock and pain would recede. He was pretty sure he'd been whacked like that at school. And there was no problem now. Was there?

The PA music recommenced. Conversations elsewhere in the club continued. Through the window, he could see people walking past, doing their shopping, waiting for buses, talking on their phones. Life was going on. He resumed his own conversation with Satan, and tried to make it sound like a bemused theoretical inquiry.

'When would you do this?'

'In the middle of the night. No one would see, and no one would see me afterwards.'

'No. I mean when? Next week? Next month?'

Satan thought about it a moment.

'When's your birthday?'

'December 28th.'

'Then that's when I'd do it.'

'You mean, December this year?'

'Yes.'

Anthony thought about his children: there was Mark and Adrian, fifteen and thirteen. His youngest child was Jonathan, ten years old. Surely he could ask for a few more years: let him grow up, toughen up?

'No….could you do it in say, three years' time?'

Satan thought about it for a moment, then nodded.

'All right. December 28th in three years' time. You get the Oscar; I hit your youngest. Do we have a deal?'

He put out his left hand to shake. Trembling, Anthony put his out too, and paused.

'Well, do we?'

'Yes,' said Anthony, quietly, wonderingly, and placed his hand in Satan's. Satan clasped it firmly, and then briskly walked off to the changing rooms, leaving Anthony alone.

Anthony was dizzy, jittery. He seemed to be buzzing all

over. Buzzing, buzzing, buzzing. It wasn't for some minutes that he realised it was his mobile phone, which he had set to vibrate. He took it out, with fumbling fingers. The number being flashed up was unfamiliar to him.

'Anthony!'

'Yes?'

'Anthony, it's Alan!'

'Alan?'

'Alan! Alan Burlington – your fucking agent!'

Flustered, Anthony laughed.

'Sorry, Alan, yes of course. How can I help?'

'How can you help? You can help by writing more scripts like this one. The phone's been ringing off the hook today! I've got three separate Hollywood studios bidding for it, and each of them's got a thick, straining, pinkish-purple hard-on a yard long! I'm getting emails saying it's fabulous, wonderful, outstanding, brilliant, every kind of superlative you can think of!'

'Today? It's all happening now? But they've had that script since last August!'

'I know. I know. Go figure. *Va savoir.* Anyway, we need to take a meeting this Friday.'

'You need me in Soho on Friday? I have to pick up the kids.'

'I don't need you on Friday in Soho. Friday, Anthony my darling, is when I need you in Los Angeles, California.'

The sudden and amazing change in Anthony's fortunes affected Beth a great deal. Suddenly, it was she who had to take time away from the office to pick the children up from school. Her husband's bruising round the face – which he explained away as a fall in the gym – soon faded. He no longer loped and moped around the house. He dynamically took meetings, agreed to script revisions, advised on directors. Beth listened to telephone conversations which habitually ended with Anthony slamming the phone down, not in rage or frustration but pure, joyful exuberance. That trip to Los Angeles was one of many. And Beth was expected to change her schedule to fit round his.

The children felt his absence most of all. His two eldest, Mark and Adrian, were boisterous types who loved football, and teasing and torturing Anthony by forcing their un-sporty dad to join in with kickabouts in the garden. But their father was now permanently unavailable. His youngest, ten-year-old Jonathan, was a bit of an accidental addition to the family – the happy result of a romantic break in Paris, and Beth, a cradle Catholic, had actually always wanted a large family; of course she was pining for a girl but loved gentle Jonathan best of all. Like Beth, Jonathan was artistic and musical. He loved dressing-up games. He suffered from migraines. He had read *Ivanhoe*. Jonathan would often come to his dad for a cuddle. But now Anthony wasn't there. Before bedtime, Jonathan would wander into his parents' bedroom, and Beth realised that it was Anthony he wanted to chat to. But Anthony was away, or out in the garden-shed-slash-office, writing.

They had much more money. Anthony seemed to be getting advances all the time. They hired two nannies, and Beth's office problems receded. They went on expensive holidays and weekend breaks. The mortgage was paid off – almost casually. Anthony, it seemed to Beth, was changing all the time. Her gloomy, morose husband was disappearing, to be replaced by the dynamic, funny, fascinating man she'd known when they were both in their twenties.

But there was something else.

Anthony, who had always been a muddled liberal, now kept bringing the conversation around to corporal punishment, and how it was no bad thing. At one of the many dinner parties he now hosted, for increasingly important and glamorous people in the film business, he always somehow managed to bring up the topic of getting the cane, or the slipper, and how it was no big deal, and really children needed a few hard knocks to prepare them for life. Many of his guests would nod sagely, but his wife would often look at him perplexed, especially when he claimed that he himself had often been beaten and it just meant nothing at all.

'What on earth was that about?' Beth asked, after one such gathering. 'You've never told me about being caned at school before? And beaten up outside the pub when you were fifteen?'

Anthony merely shrugged and said he'd only just remembered; it didn't affect him, and that was the point. With the children, too, he was different. The kickabouts with Mark and Adrian were reinstated, only now they were knockabouts – rough games of rugby in which he insisted on involving poor little Jonathan, tackling him hard, and affecting a hearty laugh when Jonathan fell over, burst into tears and ran into the arms of his appalled mother.

His film – actually a version of *Caring* – went into production with miraculous speed. They had wondered about approaching Melissa Entwhistle for the lead, but had difficulty contacting her and were given to understand she was taking a break from acting. As it was, the action was transposed to the United States, with hot young American stars in the leading roles, and the movie was, almost immediately, a colossal critical and commercial success. A string of prizes led, inevitably, to the announcement of Academy Award nominations: *Caring* had five, including one for Anthony personally, for Best Adapted Screenplay. He received the news just after lunch and the family celebrated with champagne, and Anthony attempted to tousle little Jonathan's hair with baffling roughness and negligence, leading, yet again, to his youngest bursting into tears.

'Go away! I hate you!' he shouted.

These were the last words Jonathan was ever to say to his father.

Anthony and Beth went on their own to Los Angeles for the Oscars, leaving the children behind with Beth's parents. The whole occasion passed as if in a delightful dream. It was like going to a wedding, a little like going to their own wedding. When Anthony's name was read out as they sat together, no one at all was surprised, and Anthony managed the hugs, the kisses and the run-up to the stage with enormous aplomb, giving one of the best and wittiest speeches anyone could remember. His final tribute to Beth was accompanied by a television cutaway to his wife's beaming, tearful face.

That night, in their palatial suite at the Four Seasons, Anthony and Beth did something they had not done for a long, long time. They made love. They made deep, passionate, intimate love. And afterwards, lay happily staring up in the darkness.

'That was lovely,' sighed Beth.

'Mm,' yawned Anthony.

'But you're so naughty!' giggled Beth.

'Am I? Why?'

'You didn't use a condom. Wouldn't it be sort of wonderful if I got pregnant again?'

There was a silence in the darkness.

'Beth…' asked Anthony.

'Yes?'

'If you did get pregnant, when would be the due date?'

Beth did some mental calculations and then laughed. 'December 27th. The day before your birthday!'

Kay Bruscha, former assistant to theatre producer Stephen O'Riordan, noticed that she was the only professional associate who attended Anthony's funeral. No one else in the theatre or cinema world cared to come. They had been shocked and disgusted by what had happened. The body had been discovered beside that of his day-old baby daughter, whose own demise had been triggered by a mysterious blow. Had Anthony been murderously maddened by the baby's screaming and then made away with himself? It had been known to happen. He had been reportedly catatonic with depression throughout the pregnancy. Anthony was considered a virtual non-person, erased from history.

Kay looked around at the all-but-deserted church. Anthony's widow and three sons huddled at the front, with some other relatives. She was on her own at the back: at least, she thought she was alone. Kay had really only come because she wanted to make contacts. Setting out on her own as a theatre producer was going very badly. She needed to network. But failure was staring her in the face. And here, in the church's terrible discomfort, Kay felt the authentic chill of showbusiness.

THE LOOKING GLASS

When she was twenty-two years old and fresh out of university, Natasha Gould landed the job of a lifetime. Nothing she did for the rest of her career in television ever had the emotional force and personal significance of that extraordinary first gig. Natasha was employed as a researcher for a TV company making a stunt comedy show, specialising in candid-camera hoaxes. One raucous Friday night, they set up in a London nightclub and built an entire, fake ladies' room, bisected by an enormous sheet of plate glass that ran behind a row of specially constructed handbasins. On one side of the room, they built an entire replica bathroom with a row of stalls with working lavatories. And on the other side of the glass, they built the entire thing in reverse, handbasins, towels, soap dispensers and all, so that the glass itself looked as it was a mirror, and the 'mirror' side of the glass was more brightly lit, so that no reflection would be seen. They had hired twins – two young women – to stand either side of the glass, facing each other, their movements in strictly drilled coordination, like a single person fixing her makeup. Then, when a very drunk woman came in, an 'Out Of Order' sign would be quickly placed on the closed door behind her and other clubbers directed to another genuine toilet down the corridor.

With concealed cameras cruelly recording every moment, this poor woman would be horrified when she realised that she didn't cast a reflection. The 'real-world' twin, speaking with the mirror-image silently mouthing the words, would suggest that she was maybe a vampire or her soul was corrupt; she would suggest they repeat an ancient Transylvanian spell together to lift the curse, and the poor girl would recite it, saucer-eyed with fear. She was told to do a little exorcism dance and, obedient and terrified, she would do it.

Then the production company would break the illusion. The famous bearded host would barge grinningly into the room; the mirror twin would come round to show it was all a trick and the victim would burst out laughing, hardly less astonished by her proximity to television celebrity than she had been by the supernatural disappearance of her image in the mirror. It was Natasha's job to get this dazed clubber's signature on a contract giving them the rights to show this humiliation on television. She had to do this quickly, before indignation or second thoughts set in. They were also signing for a cash fee of one hundred pounds, offered then and there, to seal the deal.

The next month, the company decided to repeat the trick, and Natasha suggested an idea to refine the torture. Everything was set up as before, only there was no glass. Just a huge rectangular space. The first person to blunder in was a young man, who hadn't realised it wasn't the men's room, but the door shut behind him and entry sealed to others in the same way. Natasha saw that this bewildered, innocent man was completely gorgeous.

He immediately saw there was something strange about the non-mirror, and wonderingly approached it.

'Where is my...? My reflection...? What's wrong with the mirror...?' he asked the twin, who said, 'Nothing!' and knocked her right fist against her image-twin's left, while Natasha – hardly able to stifle her giggles – knocked on a sheet of glass behind the wall to create the simultaneous sound effect.

The poor man looked back at the mysterious void in front of him. Then he put his hand out to it, like a blind man feeling the way, and realised that his fingers were going all the way through. With a gasp, and then a giggle, he climbed up on to the handbasin (to Natasha's alarm, as it was only a chipboard construct, and unlikely to take his weight for long), then clambered over and jumped down the other side, freezing there in a simian crouch. Like the professionals they were, the twins reacted in strict coordination: the mirror-twin on his side looking back at him, the real-twin turned the other way, looking at nothing.

Slowly standing, his face lit up with pure ecstatic joy. 'Oh my God!' he breathed. 'That pill. That fucking pill. I've actually gone through the... Through the...'

He laughed hysterically, but then the laughter turned to sobbing. Natasha looked uneasily at the producer and host who were both watching on a monitor. The producer looked back at Natasha and then gave a small, decisive head-shake, and drew his fingertips across his Adam's apple. They had to abandon the stunt. This guy was having some sort of nervous breakdown. It wasn't good television. They could get sued. Now Natasha had to spring into action.

She bustled forward and helped this man up, offered him a bottle of water and walked him through a discreet rear exit and into a corridor, while the production crew sealed off the fake room.

'Are you OK, mate?' she asked. 'What's your name?'

'Rob,' he said quietly, like a child. 'I thought… I thought I'd gone through…'

'Have you necked any pills tonight, Rob?' asked Natasha, with a wise smile.

'Well, yes, I, suppose I…have.' Rob smiled at her, abashed, sobering up. Natasha realised again how attractive he was. 'What happened back there?' he asked.

'Oh, nothing,' smiled Natasha, evasively. 'I think you were having too much of a good time. Look, let's get you home. I'll get you a taxi. Are you with anyone? Did you have a coat?'

Rob shook his head and submissively took Natasha's proffered hand as she led him down the passage – exchanging a brief glance with her producer to indicate: all under control.

Natasha and Rob walked out into the car park and round onto a busy main road in East London. There were no black cabs. Natasha got her phone out and ordered an Uber. Soon a white Toyota Prius arrived. They both got in and the car pulled away.

Rob was smiling benignly at Natasha and she smiled back.

'Thank you for helping me,' he murmured and Natasha, suppressing a twinge of guilt, said: 'Think nothing of it.'

'Shouldn't I give the driver my address?' he asked, smiling, still gazing into her eyes.

'We're going to mine,' said Natasha. They kissed for the entire twenty-minute journey.

Natasha and Rob moved in together six months after that, and became engaged three years later. He was a trainee architect, making his way in a forward-thinking young firm; Natasha rose to be producer on a crime drama about a brilliant forensic pathologist with an addiction to online poker. They would often tell friends about their bizarre first meeting. She had been in a club, she said, and went into the ladies' loos to discover Rob, off his head, crouched down, gibbering and crying, having taken a dodgy pill. None of her friends knew of her association with the programme, and never guessed that this might not be the whole story.

Natasha often thought about telling Rob the truth. But as time went by, there seemed no opportunity to do it, and it seemed less and less relevant to their busy and satisfying lives.

Yet one thing did occasionally remind her of that fateful deception: their mutual addiction to selfies. She loved taking photographs of her own face, looking upwards at the phone in the approved manner, so that the image was as flattering as possible. It was much better than a mirror image. Rob did the same, having no small sense of what a good-looking man he was. They took selfies together. They took selfies separately. They each developed very impressive followings on Instagram. They even considered opening a joint Instagram account but decided against it, as it might dilute the impressive online profiles they had each built up individually.

The day of their wedding dawned, and it was a glorious summer's day. Natasha and Rob had hired a sumptuous country hotel in Scotland: a huge event for their families and friends. An hour before the ceremony, Natasha was led into a special room in the hotel for dressing and last-minute preparation with her two bridesmaids, both dressed exactly alike – her best friend and maid-of-honour Stephanie, and her niece Elizabeth, who was just thirteen. It was a white octagonal space with no windows. There was lively chatter about what it was going to be like to spend the rest of one's life with just one person. Elizabeth, with her weird young solemnity, told Steph and Natasha how important it was to be completely honest with your husband.

'Let's do a photo!' said Natasha, and reached for her phone, which she clicked into camera mode, held out and prepared her arch, wide-eyed camera face: not a duck pout, but a lips-parted, slightly sexy expression that she knew was going to look good, especially framed by her wedding veil, and with the correct filters.

But something was wrong. Her face was gone. It had disappeared. There was nothing but the Instagram square of white. A glowing, rippling sheen of nothingness. Where was her head? Where was her face? A queasy rush took her back to an all-but-forgotten memory. Was she a vampire? Would she have to do the little exorcism dance?

Her hand shook as it held out the phone, but she nonetheless kept it in position. She started to cry.

'Where's my face?' she said. 'Oh my God, where's my face?'

'What?' Stephanie ducked in next to her and looked up at the phone and she, too, was baffled at their non-appearance.

'Oh for God's sake,' sighed Elizabeth, taking the phone off her aunt. 'You haven't got it in selfie mode. It's photographing what's ahead of you. The ceiling!'

Stunned, Natasha switched her phone off without taking the picture. Then, without another word, she walked out of the dressing suite, and down the corridor in her wedding gown to where she knew her bridegroom Rob would himself be preparing his clothes. She came in to find him doing his tie in the bathroom mirror.

'Darling!' he said, looking round from his reflection to her ashen face. 'It's bad luck to—'

'Rob,' she interrupted. 'I've got something to tell you.'

GHOSTING

After a demanding day, Gil Harris liked to absent himself from family life as long as possible once he had returned from work by remaining in the ground-floor study in his home right up until supper time. He was ostensibly catching up with correspondence, but really he was just surfing the internet, and it was while scrolling through the website of a national newspaper that he learned of the death of a young woman with whom, some years earlier, he had been casually involved.

The name 'Faye Almoner' jumped out of the screen at him: it had to be her. She had apparently been hit by a huge SUV on a pedestrian crossing, having reportedly stepped into the road too soon and given the driver insufficient time to stop. This was disputed by Faye's own family in the subsequent civil case. She had died instantly, of horrific skull injuries. If it had been a smaller car, she might have survived.

Gil googled the name to find other reports of the same incident and one from a local news outlet showed a photograph of Faye. Yes. Shorter hair, and a thinner face but definitely, yes; her.

Faye Almoner. Gil had a strange, cold, sinking feeling which, with atypical insight, he recognised as something other than compassion.

They had been together for just a few weeks. It was before he was married. He swiped right on her; they met at a bar in North London and went back to her place. It was as exciting and uncomplicated as that. She was a drama student and aspiring playwright and he was a corporate lawyer.

She was attractive and funny in a spiky way, but they had precisely nothing in common. Gil saw that. He thought she saw that too. It was just a non-serious thing. A physical thing. A fun thing. But after a while, just as Gil was beginning to wonder if they shouldn't cool it, Faye asked him if he wanted to go travelling in Europe with her over the summer, culminating in a longish stay at the Spanish farmhouse belonging to her mother and stepfather.

Gil told her his firm wouldn't let him have that much time off.

Something else happened. Gil never stayed over in Faye's room in her shared house, preferring to go back to his flat. But one night he fell asleep and woke at 2am to find her gazing at him. The intimacy unnerved Gil – as did something he had never noticed before: a poster on her bedroom wall of Charlie Brown and Snoopy from the Peanuts cartoon, apparently cut from a magazine or comic book, perhaps by Faye herself.

Gil decided to break up with Faye and thought the simplest way was just not to reply to any more of her texts or calls and block her on social media; he was actually using the 'burner' phone he kept for this kind of hook-up. In the next few weeks, he calmly reviewed the increasingly desperate, angry and wounded texts and voice notes Faye sent him but knew the thing to do was hold his nerve and not reply. Finally, she stopped trying to contact him, and for Gil it felt like the resolution to some sort of dispute with his Uber driver.

That was seven years ago, just before he met the woman to whom he was now married with a young daughter, living in a handsome house made possible by a cash gift from his parents-in-law.

Gil brooded over the story – in which Faye was described as a supermarket assistant manager – and closed the laptop smartly when his wife put her head round the door of his study, asking if he had remembered to pick up some Pecorino on the way home.

He had.

Their family dinner was always exhausting and that night Gil told his wife Alice he was going to bed early; she said yes, sure, she wanted to stay up and watch the late-night news.

Gil got into his pyjamas, crawled tiredly beneath the duvet and fell instantly asleep.

He woke some hours later, disturbed by a shift in the mattress level and a distinct coldness in the bedroom. Someone was sitting on the bed on his side, looking at him. Gil was unable to move, aside from craning his neck up from the pillow and opening his mouth. He was unable to speak and unable to swallow.

As he stared ahead, his eyes got used to the gloom and he could make out a gaunt figure with a damaged skull, silhouetted against the faint coronet of yellow light coming through the curtain from the street lamp outside.

She was crying softly and leaned forward to kiss Gil, but there was only a cratered void on the front of her face where her lips should have been. As her head approached his, he could not scream, even when the shattered edges of her broken skull scuffed his chin and forehead. He went back into a deep sleep and awoke remembering nothing.

Gil and Alice took their daughter Annie to a farmer's market the following day in a nearby school playground, where a Punch and Judy show was laid on by a local children's entertainer. Then it was lunch at a café and back home, where Annie could play with a visiting friend or possibly nap, although she seemed to be giggling excitedly about something she had videoed on his iPhone.

Gil had work he needed to catch up on. Alice did some gardening. Alice's parents came round for dinner that evening and Gil was abstracted, withdrawn, troubled by a memory of something just out of his mind's reach. Again he was exhausted, but now felt uneasy and anxious; somehow, he saw, these feelings were tied up with going to bed.

How absurd. What was he worried about?

That night he woke up again, and again he was paralysed, unable to speak or move or swallow. His wife slept on beside him, heedless. The figure with the shattered skull was now seated closer to him: from the centre of her catastrophic cranio-facial injuries she seemed to be trying to speak, or trying to cry, or trying to sing: a single keening monosyllable half way between 'You' and 'Why'. Imploringly, she reached out to Gil and he could see the fresh, livid, abrasion wounds on her forearms from where she had been briefly dragged along the tarmac under the vehicle. These arms began to snake around his neck; he felt the ripped and chafed skin and again the half-face closed against his own and muffled his silent scream.

Sunday morning saw the Harris family attend church, having revived the Anglicanism of Gil's childhood to give Annie, as he and his wife solemnly assured each other, a 'choice' about what to believe in her own future adult life, but also to get her into the excellent Church of England faith school just five minutes' drive from their house. After the service was a Sunday roast, another institution that they wanted to anchor into Annie's existence, and that week Gil found himself in the kitchen helping out, rather than retreating to his study.

He couldn't understand why he felt so numbed, so blank: a floating, drifting detachment in which, though functioning and alert, he had the odd feeling of being outside himself, looking at his body and its movements from some high vantage point. And yet Alice did not seem to notice anything amiss. He knew that there was something out of reach, out of sight – something that he was not thinking about. After lunch, Annie gigglingly busied herself with whatever nonsense she was up to on his iPhone and Gil grumpily demanded it back.

Lying down in bed that evening, he did not feel that he had fallen asleep at all, but with the jarring suddenness of a smoke alarm going off, the fear he had been suppressing and the memory of what had happened over the last two nights, flashed once more into his mind. The bedroom was lighter now, and he could see more clearly the young woman who had appeared again at the bottom of the bed, her crushed body squeezed into a Snoopy T-shirt, her head a ragged half-moon of agony. Wailing, she snaked up towards him and her bruised, distorted hands crept down the front of his pyjama bottoms.

Gil screamed.

The bedroom light snapped on. Looking wildly around, Gil saw Annie in her pyjamas; she had clearly just hopped off the bed holding his phone, her lower lip wobbling. He turned to Alice who was blearily sitting up, wearing a sheepish apologetic smile.

'Oh Gil, I'm sorry, please don't be cross,' said Alice, holding an arm out for Annie to come round to her side for a reassuring cuddle. 'I suppose I shouldn't have let her do it. She's been in here the last couple of nights, videoing you.'

'Videoing me? Why?'

'To prove something, Daddy,' said Annie in a quiet yet decided little voice.

'Prove what?'

'To prove that you've been snoring!' she said, now with a confident note of triumph.

Gil took the proffered phone from Annie and squinted at the three separate videos of his sleeping face in murky closeup, squashed against the pillow, his lips unattractively puckered as he was indeed snoring very loudly. Deciding that being a good sport was the right thing to do, though feeling coerced by his wife's complicity, Gil forced his mouth into an indulgent smile.

'Oh all right Annie,' he said, 'you're right. You've got me. I was snoring. I'm sorry. Snoring. I'll try not to. Now back to bed with you!'

Gil's tolerant amusement at Annie's cheeky prank, though strained at first, in fact became perfectly genuine over the next few days, as he repeatedly watched the videos at the office. In dull moments between meetings, and over a sandwich lunch at his desk, he smiled over the silly but amusing videos, and was rather proud of his daughter's ingenuity and boldness. On the train in the morning and on the way home in the afternoon, he would take his phone out and, with his earphones in, he would watch the hilarious footage. He just couldn't seem to tire of it.

Even at home, Annie's silly nocturnal videos became the thing he liked to watch in his study-slash-office. And when Alice took Annie away for an overnight trip to her parents in Wales, he found he was watching them all the time, although what he initially assumed was a wi-fi fault one evening rather spoiled his final viewing.

He pressed play but instead of snoring, his pictured face just lay there, silent and immobile, the lips pressed together. Had the video stopped? Was it buffering? Now he saw that his eyes, which had been closed every other time he had watched this video, were wide open and staring blankly back at him, or rather at something just over his shoulder. The lips opened and emitted a wail, just as Gil felt the temperature in the room cooling. Faye's blood-stained fingers curled around both sides of his face, grasped the sides of his mouth and pulled and pulled and pulled, until the skin ripped away from his jaw and his own cries became entirely inaudible.

FAT FINGER

At 10:40 on a Friday night, Ali thumbed out this text message on her phone:

Hi - our lovely pilates instructor russell wants to work on my core strength but I'd rather he took me to an ibis and fucked my brains out

She had Russell's number and her plan was a radical ice-breaker: to send the message accidentally-on-purpose to him rather than to its ostensible recipient, her friend and co-worker Maya. But she accidentally-for-real sent it to her husband Malcolm instead, and three years later she was divorced, living in an entirely different city and teaching Pilates herself.

Ali had rented studio space from another instructor, Zuleika, who had converted the lower floor of the terraced house in which she now lived on her own after a recent divorce. This was basically a large room with parquet-style flooring on which crash mats could be placed in various positions. There were mirrors around the surrounding walls, rather like a ballet studio without a barre, and even some mirrors on the ceiling so that clients could assess their form while in the prone position. A water-cooler stood in the corner. A stack of unread and out-of-date glossy magazines was placed in the opposite corner – a bad idea of Zuleika's which made the place look inappropriately like a hairdresser's. Ali had the space on Mondays and Thursdays, with Zuleika using it the rest of the week, for a weekly rent which Ali frankly felt was more appropriate to three or four days a week. Moreover, Zuleika's sessions actually overlapped with Ali's at the end of the day on Thursday. She had a client at one end of the studio at that time, while Ali was with one of hers at the other.

Relying on a modest advertisement in the local press, some word of mouth, and an industrious use of social media, Ali soon had a reasonable client base, quite equal to that of Zuleika, who couldn't help noticing the fact that Ali had achieved this success despite being a relative newcomer. For her part, Ali couldn't help noticing that though she herself accepted payment by cheque, by direct debit to her bank account and also by PayPal, Zuleika accepted only cash, and was prepared to make an off-the-record discount on that basis. Cash was also how she wanted the rent to be paid.

Ali and Zuleika got on perfectly well. They said 'Hiya' when they saw each other and asked how each other's weekends had been, or were likely to be.

The problem arose when a new client came: James, an investment banker. He was one of Ali's.

James was in his late fifties, overweight, recently divorced himself. He said he suffered from back pain, leg pains, and knee pains. He was convinced that Pilates was the answer to his problems. Ali did her best, boldly combining Pilates with a kind of physiotherapy.

'How is that?' she would ask, manipulating his knee joint.

'Oh…um…wonderful,' winced James, with a thoughtful expression.

Yet he professed himself extremely happy at the end of every session, and in fact insisted on paying Ali two or three times the agreed fee. It was an apparently impulsive gesture which Ali didn't mind.

However, when he began to sweat – which he did almost immediately after the Pilates instruction had begun – James gave off an overpowering smell. It was quite disgusting. But Ali felt that she should not mention it. James was clearly aware of it himself. After the fourth session, he unilaterally quadrupled the fee, apparently in shame at his body odour.

At the beginning of the fifth session, which was on a Thursday – the 'overlap' time – Zuleika wandered casually over to where Ali was working with James, with a snowy white towel around her neck and drinking some ion-enriched mineral water.

'That's great, James!' she said. 'Good work.'

This was an unthinkable error of taste on her part – an appalling breach of protocol and good manners – to start butting in on someone else's session. Ali felt her cheeks burn with rage as she crouched over James. When they finished, Zuleika was still there, perched on a stool in the corner, casually looking at something on her phone. James offered the usual quadruple fee, but Ali rather coldly insisted that she wanted to take only the agreed sum. She got changed quickly in the little adjoining room and walked out to the bus stop, leaving James behind to chat with Zuleika.

Two days later, Ali received the following text:

Hi Zuleika – how u doin? I was thinking about what u said. Ali is such a wonderful person and a wonderful pilates instructor. It's just that she is not right for me. Her hands are too big. I'm sure that she doesn't want to teach me anyway. I want to change to being your client. But she is such a wonderful, lovely person, it's just that I can't think of a way to tell her I want to change pilates teachers. James

Ali pondered this message for some considerable time. Later that afternoon, James received the following text:

Hi Zuleika — how are you? We didn't really have a chance to talk today but I wondered if you had any advice for me. My client James smells, he gets erections when I manipulate his knee joints and he has wandering hands. I think that deep down he may be a nice person but there is something dodgy about him. What do you think I should do about this? Yours, Ali

Two hours went by and then Ali received this text:

Hi Zuleika — just to say that when we are married, I think I want to take a closer interest in the running of the Pilates business, I think you should rationalise it to just you offering the service, so we can't have Ali in there with her great big hands and pudgy fingers. She's got to go. Love, James

Immediately afterwards, Zuleika received this text:

Dear Sir/Madam: I hope that this is the right 'text-hotline' for the HMRC tax evasion unit. This is just to say that my colleague, Zuleika Pearce of 141 Quex Road, London NW6, has been continuously accepting payments in cash for her Pilates business and so owes a very great deal in unpaid tax. Yours ever, Ali Stevenson

The following morning, Ali received this text:

Dear James, I'm sorry to have to say this to you by text but I'm afraid on reflection I cannot accept you as a client, and your offer of marriage, though gallant, is also not workable. You will have to return to being Ali's client — and she is an excellent instructor. Yours ever, Zuleika Pearce

But James did not return and Zuleika and Ali went back to their other clients, although, from that moment on, there was no overlap in their schedules.

SRSLY

For two years, Alan had worked for a media company based in East London which streamed quality content to subscribers' smartphones, tablets and PlayStation consoles. He was good at his job, but in the past four months, his line manager Siobhan had seemed considerably more impressed with the work being done by a new hire: Justin – a 21-year-old, technically junior to Alan but with a beard longer than Tolstoy's, and of the same rich chestnut colour as his hair, which, though worn casually long, did not obscure the Celtic cross tattoo on his neck. As for Alan, he was almost entirely bald, with a straggly ring of reddish hair around the back of his head, and a small, flat, pug-like nose. At the last strategy meeting, Siobhan had listened with intensely focused respect to Justin's comments on the possibility of covering the indoor snowboarding championships in Cluj. But when Alan interjected a perfectly good idea about sponsorship and brand synergy, Siobhan stopped smiling and looked at Alan as if he had food on his chin.

One Saturday morning, Alan found himself in Starbucks, nursing a latte and a sense of resentment. His daily headache throbbed insidiously through his jaw and sinuses. He found himself compulsively checking out Justin's X/Twitter feed on his phone. This featured comments about streaming media, which were always being liked and retweeted by Siobhan.

It wasn't long before Alan saw something that made his entire body clench with irritation. Justin was taking part in a popular social media game which involved the participant listing six bands and challenging the reader to guess which one they hadn't seen in concert. With exquisitely annoying conceit, Justin had specified six bands of exactly equal hipster-ish cachet. It was unbelievably smug.

Almost before he knew what he was doing, Alan had placed his phone face-up on the tabletop, so that he could vigorously make the 'wanker' gesture at it with both hands, unencumbered. He did this quite unselfconsciously, in the middle of Starbucks. Any possible embarrassment at this futile display of envious rage was nullified by his realisation that the activity was relieving his headache.

He couldn't believe it at first. As a test, he stopped doing the 'wanker' gesture at Justin's tweet and the pain came back. Then he did it with just one hand, and the pain was halved.

So he continued to make the sign at Justin's annoying tweet on his phone, and not only did the pain vanish, but it soon began to be replaced with a kind of sweetness, and rapture – the sort you might get from drinking wine or smoking weed. Alan carried on industriously making the double-handed 'wanker' gesture at his phone in the middle of Starbucks, where people were beginning to notice. And despite the fact that his wrists were starting to ache, his physical sense of delight was escalating.

And then it happened.

His pleasure went to the next level. His whole body relaxed. He slumped down into his seat, his eyes rolled up into his head, his pelvis seemed to melt and his knees flopped away from each other in a manspreading pose, causing people to move along either side, while he made the double 'wanker' gesture.

At that point, Alan felt a whooshing noise inside his head; he felt as if his body were being crunched into a tiny compacted mass of just a few cubic millimetres, like a mouthful of candy floss. The whooshing noise grew in volume, then stopped abruptly, and he discovered he was on horseback, enjoying the dappled sunshine on his face, as he rode through the forest of Yakushima, in Southern Japan. He could feel how much taller and stronger he was than usual. What an imposing and lordly figure he must cut, as he sat, straight-backed, on his horse, Kazuya. The samurai armour, or *dou*, on his chest glittered in the noonday heat, though he wore no helmet above his *guruwa*, or throat protector. A large *kubi-bukuro* at his waist contained the severed head of his recently defeated enemy, which he intended to present to his master. He could smell the sharp sour tang of blood from its exposed neck and it was delicious.

He sensed immediately that he was richer than he had been before. There was no material evidence for this. He just knew from the good feeling in every limb that he must have much more money. It felt great to lean forward and give Kazuya's neck a gently affectionate caress, and know instinctively that human beings thereabouts would be as submissively respectful to him as this horse, and in that moment he began to think of himself as 'the Horseman'. He was a warrior who had defeated someone with his sword, his *katana,* with the sixty-centimetre blade which now nestled at his hip. He knew that he must have washed it in the trickling waters of a local stream before restoring it to his scabbard, or *saya,* with its exquisitely designed guard piece, or *tsuba.* A mile or so behind him, the horribly dishonoured headless corpse would be sprawled in a clearing, or perhaps he had contemptuously hung it from a bough. He couldn't quite remember for the moment.

Man and horse cantered onwards. The Horseman felt as if he could continue like this forever. There was something so glorious in the way he could exult in pure wellbeing. Until he heard a cry. At first, he took it for a bird. But then he knew it came from a woman, moaning from inside a rudimentary hut in a clearing to his left – wooden, on rough raised posts.

Instantly, he reined his horse to a halt, dismounted with athletic ease, tethered Kazuya loosely to a bush and approached the hut on foot. The moaning grew clearer and louder, and the silences between each pained gasp more emphatic. He grasped the door's wooden screen, slid it firmly to the side, and entered, not scrupling to remove his boots.

Immediately he could see the woman on a low bed, quite alone, a bowl, or *donburi hachi,* next to her full of steaming hot water. A rough coverlet covered her distended stomach and it was clear that she was in the throes of childbirth. The difficulty of the labour and the fact that there were no other children in the hut indicated that this was her first child. But where was her husband? And where was the nursemaid or doctor who had to superintend this whole business? The woman's cries were unbearable. Her labour would need to be induced. And he knew the only way to bring this about: intercourse.

It was at this moment that the whinnying of his horse outside signalled the arrival of a visitor; or rather, it was the master of the house who now entered – a cringingly insecure-looking young man who was with an elderly low-born woman, evidently the midwife, whom he had clearly gone to fetch, but to whom he seemed unbecomingly deferential, even in these circumstances.

This man demanded, though in a cracked, uncertain voice, who the Horseman was and what he was doing in the hut with the man's pregnant wife. The Horseman replied casually that he thought he might be able to help, but would now leave. The man barred his way. In response to this, he coolly indicated that he had wished merely to be of assistance and now wished to leave, but expressed this in a casual, high-handed way, and moreover did not look the young man in the eye, but rather directed his glance at a spot in his forehead, an insulting mannerism that might have gone unremarked, were it not for the fact that he had his hand on his sword.

For a few blank, tense moments, no words passed between the two men, and the only sound was the pregnant woman's whimpering. Then the husband placed his hand on the interloper's chest, and was in reply struck across the face with an open hand. The old midwife, evidently quite accustomed to chaotic scenes, prepared to busy herself with the impending birth, which could yet be many hours away.

The husband reeled backwards out of the door, clutching his face, snivelling pathetically, and the Horseman followed him with swift, sure strides, but without unsheathing his sword. He merely grasped the man by his ragged waistband

and by the scruff of his neck, picked him up bodily with hardly a gasp of effort, and marched over to the nearby trickling stream, where he intended to give the man a salutary douche for his impertinence in striking him. And as he held him over the water, he caught a glimpse of their two faces, ripplingly reflected in the surface. The husband's, with his cringing face, his straggly fringe of reddish hair around the back of his head and a small, flat, pug-like nose, and the Horseman's own, with his long, powerful beard of the same rich chestnut colour as his hair, which, though worn casually long, did not obscure the Celtic cross tattoo on his neck. The man landed in the water with an almighty splash. There was then a flutter of disturbed birds and the thin yawl of a newborn baby.

PALM TO PALM

What an ordeal the dating circuit is for older people – particularly that stabbing little moment of disillusion at the very start of the evening when your date walks into the restaurant and you recognise their face from the website photo and yet see that it's older and less attractive than the picture…and realise they are thinking exactly the same thing about your face.

But for Simon, a divorced man in his fifties, things were going extraordinarily well. He was having dinner with Miriam, who was a little older than him, dressed elegantly and simply, hair cut in a stylish gamine grey bob. She was a widow, and employed as a proofreader in a publishing house. Simon himself was a solicitor.

They talked genially about their mutual reluctance to retire and their love of travel. Miriam had journeyed by train down through South America to Tierra del Fuego; Simon had driven through central Europe and had had an enthusiastic response to his subsequent whimsical blog about Bulgarian nightlife. There had been talk of publication or a slot on Radio 4. Miriam was enthusiastic and encouraging.

A second bottle of wine was ordered in the middle of the main course and they talked about a subject that was never far away for people of their age: losing their elderly parents. Miriam's mother was in a care home, suffering from dementia. Her father was dead. Simon's father had died when he was four years old; he had no siblings and his mother brought him up as a single parent in a single-bedroom flat in West London. She had a vanishingly small income from his dad's inadequate pension but they got by well enough. Simon's mother, who lived in this same flat until the very end, had died two months previously, and telling Miriam this caused tears to spring to his eyes. Impulsively, Miriam reached across the table and took his hand and they just stayed like this, hand in hand, for quite some time. It was the nearest thing to human contact either of them had had for years.

Without letting go, Simon playfully turned Miriam's palm over and began to trace the lines on it with his fingertip.

'You know, my mother was a great palm reader.'

'Really?'

'Yes!' Simon laughed quietly, almost to himself. 'She was renowned for it. Although she said that it was always more revealing to read the palm of someone of the opposite sex. And I think I inherited her powers.'

'Is that right?' said Miriam, not withdrawing her hand and allowing the conversation to settle into this new flirtatious mode.

'Yes. It's a funny thing. When my mum first told me she was a palm reader I was eleven. I borrowed books from the library and learned all about it, just to be closer to her.'

Simon continued to gaze into Miriam's palm, apparently for a moment lost in thought.

'Well, what does my palm tell you?' asked Miriam, keen to continue this agreeably romantic turn to the conversation.

Simon looked up, smiled, as if awakened from a reverie, and then looked down again.

'Is this your dominant hand?' he asked.

'Yes,' said Miriam, obscurely stirred by this technical inquiry.

'Well you have a long, strong arc on your lifeline, clear, defined and well away from the thumb.'

'Is that good?'

'It's very good. It means you are a strong, vibrant person. Are you good at sports?'

'I'm really good at squash.'

'That's exactly what I was going to say. Now your heartline. The one at the top running horizontally across. This is very interesting.'

'What's so interesting about it?'

'Well, it starts under the middle finger, as opposed to the forefinger.'

'And what does that tell you?'

'It tells me you tend to be more concerned with your own happiness than your partner's, and in sexual terms, that you are more concerned with your own pleasure than your partner's.'

This audacious remark was greeted with a tiny silence, but Miriam began to caress the top of Simon's wrist with her thumb.

'I wouldn't say that was true exactly,' she murmured.

'You have two money lines,' said Simon, 'and they both begin at the base point of your lifeline. That means you have more than one professional interest and they are both very successful.' They both took a moment to recall Miriam telling him she was an editor as well as a proofreader.

'Your headline, under the heartline, is excellent: really long and clear. But what's this?'

'What?' asked Miriam, for a moment absurdly worried by the theatrical note of dismay that Simon had playfully adopted.

'The headline has a certain waviness. Do you see?' She saw. 'That means you are occasionally too easily distracted. And as for this marriage line, the one under your little finger...well, goodness.'

'What? *What?*' asked Miriam, now thoroughly entranced.

'I can see two of them. That means that at some time in your life you were in love with two people at the same time. Were you?'

Now entirely awestruck, and sipping wine with the other hand, Miriam found that it was her turn to be entirely lost in thought. 'Yes,' she said quietly. 'Yes I was.'

Simon judged this to be the moment to release her hand.

'Well,' said Miriam, taking yet another gulp. 'Your mother seems to have taught you very well.'

'Ha!' said Simon. 'Actually, she didn't teach me. Not really. In fact, she was a bit cagey about it. I learned everything from my little library book at the age of eleven.'

'Really?'

'Yes. Do you know, it's funny, I haven't thought about this in years. Not since I was eleven.'

'How odd!'

'Yes, I just came home early from school one day, and I

remember dumping my satchel and Mum came into the front room and there was this man with her. And he talked with Mum a bit, just by the front door, and then he went away and I asked Mum who he was and it was strange because she didn't answer me at first. But then she told me – that she was a palm reader. And every so often, I would come home early and find some chap or other who'd come round in the afternoon to have his palm read, and…'

Simon stopped talking. His memory of his mother, which for decades had been a soft blur, like Super-8 footage out of focus, snapped into sharp focus. The flat in which he had spent his childhood came back to him with vivid clarity: the wallpaper with its tiny tessellating hexagons whose shape couldn't be seen unless you put your face really close to the wall. The string across the wall in the front room which was for Christmas cards and which his mother said she couldn't be bothered to take down the rest of the year, the tiny colour television with a screen no larger than a paperback book turned sideways, the exotically decorated Chinese tin box in his mum's bedroom which she said contained the money from her palm-reader clients that she was saving up for his birthday presents.

Simon and Miriam left the restaurant soon after that and did not stay in touch.

THIS IS WHY
WE CAN'T HAVE
NICE THINGS

Jas (he sometimes wrote it Jaz) drove an online grocery van whose one-hour delivery slots extended from seven in the morning until eleven at night. Jas found it very hard work. He had in each case to leave his vehicle with the hazards flashing so that he was not in contravention of any neighbourhood parking restrictions; he had to unload great heavy plastic crates full of food from the back and then bring them up to the front door, ring the bell and then speak with breezy but unhurried friendliness to the householder and ignore the little voice inside his head telling him to get on with it, because there was another delivery to be made, and another and another. Jas wore a green hi-vis tabard over his sweatshirt and shorts in even the coldest weather.

He would offer to bring the crates into the kitchen for the customer, and noticed how these people would never look him in the eye; they would always be concentrating on their delivery. He entered and left hundreds of London homes like a ghost.

The deliveries blurred into each other. Sometimes Jas would clock off at the end of a shift and realise that he could remember nothing of what had happened in the previous eight hours.

But there was one type of delivery that he lived for. He was not a malicious or cruel person, but his every skin-pore fizzed with excitement when he realised he had one of these: a certain type of delivery that was going to wipe the smile – or the supercilious look of superiority – from the customer's face.

It was a delivery of a half a dozen or so bottles of wine whose total cost fractionally exceeded the minimum charge, and nothing else. People would put this on their order provisionally, just to keep the slot on hold, planning to add more proper groceries later and remove the wine. But every so often they forgot and then Jas would show up with the pointless six bottles of wine – those unwanted luxury items that mocked the buyer's failure to get proper provisions. With a connoisseur's appreciation of middle-class dismay, Jas savoured first the buyers' uncomprehending astonishment that someone was ringing their doorbell so early on a Sunday morning and then their heart-sinking dismay as the memory came back to them. Theoretically, customers had the option to change their minds about any or all of the items in the crate – they could send it all back – but generally the embarrassment of admitting this complete blunder, and moreover forcing this delivery person to carry the crate back to the van, was just too great. They grumpily admitted him, while somehow trying to claim to themselves that they needed to stock up on wine anyway.

This mini-disaster cracked open their routine, and for a microsecond laid bare their lives, framed in that open front door. Jas felt at this moment that he could see them as human beings: open, naked, vulnerable. It was also the only occasion when the customers looked directly back at him.

Whistling a lively tune, he carried the crate with six clinking bottles of Picpoul de Pinet up to the front door of a Mr John Smith, and pressed hard on the doorbell.

The door opened.

'Morning!' said Jas cheerfully – adding, with exquisite insolence: 'Having a party, Mr Smith?'

This John Smith looked back at him with something Jas had never seen: a cold, blank, immobile face. He was in his pyjamas, unshaven, with dishevelled hair and an anti-snoring strip still on his nose. Usually at this stage they would look mortified. But this Mr John Smith just looked dead inside.

'Follow me,' said Mr Smith, turning on his heel and walking back down the hall. Jas followed him through a weirdly bare passageway (on his left he could see a room from which everything had been removed), and then into the kitchen, which was similarly empty. A sleeping bag on some sofa cushions in the kitchen, like a dog basket, was where Mr Smith had been lying.

Jas placed his crate on the floor (there was no kitchen table) and Mr Smith plucked out one of the bottles, unscrewed it, and putting it to his cracked and discoloured lips, had drunk about half before Jas realised what was happening. Part of the job was asking the customer to confirm that the order was all there – an enjoyably deadpan moment of pure insolence in the six-bottle cases. But Mr Smith ignored his hesitant prompting on this point, finished the bottle, threw it with a loud and jarring *clank* back into the crate, selected a second and now asked him: 'Join me?'

'No Mr Smith, I really…'

Mr Smith downed this second bottle in about the same time and emptied the third just as quickly.

'Mr Smith, can you confirm that the order is correct…?' asked Jas.

Instead of replying, Mr Smith put the unopened fourth bottle he'd been fondling back into the crate, pressed his palms to his temples and burst into tears.

There was no milk, no instant coffee, nothing for Jas to offer poor Mr Smith. But he was able to fill two empty yogurt cartons with water from the tap and hand one to his distraught customer once he had recovered his calm.

'I lost everything,' said Mr Smith. 'I had everything. But I lost it. I was able to give my wife and children everything. All the wonderful things they wanted. I had a lovely business windfall from an opportunity that came my way from Benin. You know it? But then I re-invested it in New York with someone you've probably never heard of. I lost everything. And my wife and children are gone. Soon I shall have to leave this house. I have nothing. I am sixty years old.'

Jas stirred, looked at his watch, and realised that he was now getting behind. 'Mr Smith, look, I sort of have to be going but if there's anyone you need to talk to, I'm sure you can Google some helpline numbers…'

'Google?' said Mr Smith bitterly. 'Google on what? A computer? A smartphone? I don't have any of those now and don't tell me to use my local library because I'm barred for inappropriate behaviour.'

'Oh.'

They sat in morose silence for some moments and then Mr Smith asked: 'What about what you do – do you think I could get a job doing that?'

'You mean online grocery-delivery driving?'

'Yes. I mean, how hard can it be? No offence.'

'Well...'

Mr Smith suddenly jumped up. 'Show me,' he said, decisively. 'I mean it's just like driving a car, isn't it?'

To humour him, and because he now needed to get back to work promptly, Jas allowed Mr Smith to walk back with him to the van, whose driver-side door he had left open.

'Well, Mr Smith, I've got to go, but all the b—'

Before Jas could stop him, Mr Smith had jumped into the van and sat behind the wheel.

'Come on. Hop in. Show me how it works,' he said.

Jas looked around in the empty London street, for all the world as if someone was going to get him out of this situation, or object on his behalf to what Mr Smith was doing. Then he climbed up into the passenger seat, to speak more gently and persuasively to this customer, in his pyjamas and dressing gown, gripping the wheel of his van, his face flushed, his pupils dilated, his lips drawn from back from his teeth in a peculiar, sensual grin.

'Look Mr Smith, you've got to get out now. I've let you have your fun and I feel bad for you. But please...'

'Come on. Be a sport. Let me drive this round the block just once and I won't get you into trouble for drinking with me.' Mr Smith winked at him – the first time in his adult life that Jas had witnessed this antique mannerism.

Tensely, he considered the situation.

'All right. Just around the block. Then that's it, yeah?'

'Absolutely.'

Jas let Mr Smith start the van and they drove off, but instead of taking the first left for a circular route back to their starting point, Mr Smith floored the accelerator, heading for the main road.

'If we crash, you'll be in line for an insurance pay-out,' shouted Mr Smith. 'We can split it, and then we can both afford all those things! All the wonderful things!'

And so they approached the traffic lights and the other cars, with the pedestrians looking around at them in alarm. Suddenly the morning sunlight seemed dazzlingly bright, bouncing off the bodywork of other vehicles, as the engine of Jas' van rose to a desolate wail.

'All the wonderful things!'

INTIMATE

Janice was not someone who had to dominate every conversation. She was a stylish woman with a dancer's grace and poise learned from her days on the professional stage twenty years before. She just knew how to impose her personality on the room. And there had been times (at a dinner party, say) when she'd had to pump someone's brakes: it was when they asked what it was like being an 'intimacy coach'. The term, she patiently explained, was 'intimacy co-ordinator'.

Since Weinstein, she would say – and those two words enforced a solemn, nodding, gaze-lowering silence from men who might otherwise be tempted to make jokes – her work was needed on film and television sets. Her guidance was brought in to shape a love scene. Consent and the representation of consent needed to be established. People's feelings needed to be respected not just during the scene. But before the scene. And after the scene. Janice was shepherding intimacy throughout the shoot. It was holistic. Janice would explain these ideas about her work and some of the more well-meaning men would say something like: oh yeah, it's like being a stunt choreographer. Always. They always said 'stunt choreographer'. Well, Janice would say…more like being just a straightforward choreographer. No need for the 'stunt'!

Actually, Janice's background was in choreography. She'd worked in musical theatre and dabbled in reiki healing. Her marriage ended without acrimony and without children (she hadn't wanted them) and Janice had thrown herself into her professional life even more, in the noughties producing a short film in which a love scene needed to be delicately handled. She was a natural. Soon her expertise was being called upon all the time, and in the past three years she had emerged as one of the industry's pre-eminent intimacy specialists.

Which is what made her last job so confusing. Janice was working on a high-profile feature film and she'd been called in because there was a scene showing a hotel-room encounter between two women and a man. Without Janice, that scene could have been just crass, as well as an emotional minefield. But, as everyone in the production later agreed, she handled everything superbly. First, she got the three of them (Ros, Hope and Gary) to block out the scene very approximately. Then she got them to sit down, wearing loose clothing, cross-legged in a circle, holding hands – Janice too – and they went round saying how much they loved and respected each other. Actors sometimes teased Janice for being a hippy about this, but it always helped, and her presence in the circle ventilated the emotional enclosure. Poor nervous Gary held her hand extra tightly, and gave her such a sweet smile before they began.

And then it happened. At the scene's climactic moment, with Gary having intimacy with Ros while Hope kissed him, he was supposed to break off and give an incoherent groan. But instead he gasped: 'Oh Janice…'

Everyone heard it. The director called cut, and after a stunned silence everyone burst out laughing, including Janice, and poor Gary went as red as a beetroot. Janice said: 'Not to worry, it happens all the time! It's like your first day at primary school when you call the teacher "Mum"!' That got a big laugh, which really eased the tension on set. They did the scene again and it went fine.

Janice was fibbing. It didn't happen all the time. She was reasonably sure that it was the first time it had ever happened in the history of intimacy co-ordination. An hour afterwards, Janice got a text from Gary: *I'm so sorry about my stupid mistake today! Gx*

Janice replied: *Don't worry you were superb! Jxx*

Gary: *Thanks to you! Listen: I'd love to talk to you about my solo scene. I think there's an intimacy dimension to it. Could you maybe come to my trailer around 3pm? I'm really sorry to ask! Gxxx*

Janice pondered this text for a very long time. The solo scene he was talking about was when his character, a maverick detective, goes for a run, comes back to his apartment, and while he's having a shower is assailed by a flashback of his intimate encounter with Ros and Hope, and realises that the scorpion tattoo he'd glimpsed on Hope's lower back exactly matches the one on the corpse he'd been shown the previous day in the morgue.

Janice thought to herself: well, maybe there was an intimacy implication to that shower scene. His character was very vulnerable at that moment. So was Gary himself.

Perhaps she would go and see him to consult on intimacy.

She texted back: *Sure! See you there tomorrow at 3pm*

Janice accidentally hit send before she had decided how many kissy-xs to put. The next morning and lunchtime dragged. Janice was not in fact specifically needed on set that day. She spent the time thinking how impressed and moved she was that Gary had asked for help. At ten minutes to three, she marched purposefully towards his trailer, wearing a gorgeous puffy anorak with furry hood and carrying a cardboard recessed tray with two lattes and two danishes. But just before she got there, a runner stopped her, blocking her path and holding up his palm like a traffic cop.

'I'm sorry, Janice,' he said. 'This coronavirus thing. There's a lockdown – we're suspending production and we have to take physical distancing very seriously or we're all in big trouble with the insurers. I've got a car ready to take you where you need to go, and there's a mask on the back seat if you haven't got one.'

Janice collected her bag. She wanted to give some people a hug goodbye but found everyone nervously leaning away from everyone else, as if surrounded by invisible two-metre forcefield bubbles. After literally throwing the coffee and danishes away, she found herself in the back of the cab, whose driver had already installed a plastic shield between the front and back seats, like a thick shower curtain. None of the cast or the director were to be seen. She called Gary but it went straight to voicemail and Janice was so flustered she didn't leave a message.

In the days and weeks that followed, Janice worked from

home, or rather she couldn't. Intimacy co-ordination, like nursing or cleaning, was work that couldn't be done from home. She emailed various production companies, who all told her the same thing: their projects had stalled. Theatre work was in abeyance. When she greeted her neighbour in the morning, they would normally huddle in for a chat; now they stood so far apart that they were almost projecting in stage voices.

The worst was going to the supermarket, which she could, once the lockdown had eased a little. Without thinking one morning, Janice leant forward in the checkout queue to ask someone in a mask where she had got her lovely bangle, and this person turned and literally barked: 'Two metres!' Her cheeks burning with indignation and shame, Janice straightened, looked directly ahead and was silent. She went on to develop a new way of walking around the supermarket's one-way system: slow-moving, holding the basket with her right arm out in an ostentatious diagonal maximising her width, signalling that she herself was aware of other people, and would be obliged if others would keep back.

It was while she was shopping that she saw a magazine which had a big article about the film she had been working on. They had apparently finished it all without her, including Gary's solo scene. Janice opened the magazine, and the interview inside said that Gary was going to marry Ros, who turned out to be his girlfriend. Janice was thinking about this when a voice in her ear said: 'Excuse me.' It was the 'two-metre' woman with the bangle. Like a criminal, Janice said a sharp 'sorry', put the magazine down and walked away quickly.

At home, she did Zoom calls with her mum and her sister, and spent these conversations looking at her own face. She got Government furlough help as a self-employed person. She binge-watched award-winning dramas on streaming services. She tweeted out links to her blog. She found the interview she had been reading online and pondered it some more, especially Gary's solo scene and what differences she might have made to it. She followed Gary on Instagram, but he did not follow her back.

She went back to the supermarket. The weekly shop became a daily one. Anything to break up the monotony. It felt like she could find celery or bouillon with her eyes closed. Also, she went for walks around the park, clocking up her daily ten thousand steps, according to the Fitbit on her wrist. Sometimes, when she'd only managed nine thousand eight hundred, Janice lay on the sofa eating crisps and jerkily shook her Fitbit arm two hundred times to get up to the total.

She started to cry a bit. Nothing too serious. She would cry last thing at night and sometimes at lunchtime over an abstemious bowl of gazpacho. She saw tears drop into the soup and laughed at what she imagined was the new salty flavour.

In her heart, she realised that she mustn't cry any more.

And then, in the park, it happened. Janice was sitting on a bench intended for two people, but she was right in the middle of it, effectively claiming the whole thing for herself. A very familiar voice said: 'Excuse me. Hello.'

Janice looked up sharply. It was the bangle-woman in the mask, holding what was clearly her packed lunch and standing with what a lifetime's work in the theatre told Janice was outrageously pass-agg body language.

'All right, *all right*,' she snapped. 'Look, I'm going. I'm going, all right?'

'No, no!' the woman said, pleadingly, removing her mask. 'It's me. Look!'

She removed her mask and left it dangling from one ear. It was Hope, the other woman in the three-way scene.

'Oh my God! Hope!' said Janice, and realised that her voice had gone into a weird falsetto gulp through under-use. 'I didn't know it was you! I'm so sorry!'

'No, I'm sorry!' said Hope. 'I was so stroppy and horrible that day in the supermarket. I was so stressed!'

'Oh my God, how are you?'

'I'm all right I suppose, how are you? You were so wonderful directing that scene!'

'You were so wonderful in it!'

And so Janice and Hope fell to talking on the bench, two metres apart. They lived nearby to each other; Hope lived on her own too, and they began meeting most days in the park for lunch. And somehow, one topic above all things kept recurring. Testing. What would happen if they needed to get tested? Should they get tested if they had what they thought were symptoms, but just turned out to be a cold?

Hope and Janice agreed that they quite often had sniffles which might or not be significant. It would be arguably irresponsible not to get tested. Hope travelled fifty miles to get a test at a drive-through unit. Janice actually drove into central London to get a private test done in Harley Street which cost an extravagant amount of money. As soon as possible, they met in the park and casually showed each other their negative results, and congratulated each other on this happy outcome. And then Hope asked Janice if she might like to come back to her flat for coffee, and Janice agreed.

No one was around when they went into the house. Janice

took off her puffy anorak and laid it on Hope's couch, and Hope did the same. And within the next minute, the whole question of blogging and Zoom calls and Fitbits and tweeting and going to the supermarket and eating salty soup had become entirely irrelevant.

LOYALTY

STAMP 1

Kevin De Trafford, newly single, noticed the new coffee shop immediately. It was on Piccadilly, to the left of the Royal Academy and next to the Hotel Meridien, which he walked past from the Underground station every day on his way to work.

The name was Café Fidel.

Pausing and cupping his hands over his face up against the plate glass, Kevin could see Cuban flags and a small picture of Castro over the counter. Otherwise the theme was not stressed.

Café Fidel was enormous. What had been there before?

Kevin could not remember.

Through the glass, he could see the traditional array of pastries and treats. Pains-aux-raisins. Pains-au-chocolat. Bulging muffins. Plump danishes. Single medallion-style chocolate coins, wrapped in gold paper, the size of saucers. A big laminated picture on the wall showed the surface of one of their lattes, with the 'heart' shape expertly inscribed in milky froth. Mouthwatering.

Kevin went in and joined the line of people waiting. There was a man in front of him whose label was poking up from the back of his T-shirt. The label displeased Kevin. He had a need to put the man's label back in. He could just take it between his finger and thumb and put it in. But what if his fingers touched the man's neck? Would that be construed as a sexual come-on? It was a risk worth taking, surely. He could just poke the label back down. He could imagine his fingernail accidentally scratching the man's skin as he did so. He could imagine the man turning with astonishment and anger. Or perhaps some kind of ambiguous sexual excitement.

Kevin was nearing the head of the queue. He had decided on a double, or, as Café Fidel styled it, a 'mucho' cappuccino and a sugary and lavishly proportioned Eccles cake. He checked his phone with the aid of Café Fidel's wifi password: *staunch*.

But just as the person ahead of him with the sticking-out label was about to pay for his coffee, a man with a tattoo of Cthulhu on his neck whooshed up to them both on a shiny metal scooter, which almost ran over Kevin's foot.

'You all right?' this newcomer said to the label man.

'I'm all right yeah,' he replied.

'Could you get me eight cappos for the crew?'

'Mmm.'

So Kevin's wait was to be considerably lengthened. Sure, this substantial extra order was being placed by the person ahead of him. Fair enough. There were technically no issues around queue-jumping. But Kevin reflected that he had effectively been reviewing and renewing his own intention to stay in the line on a moment-by-moment basis, premised on the idea that there was just one more single-person-sized order ahead of him.

He felt resentment.

Yet having made the decision to come into Café Fidel, Kevin decided to tough it out and stay the course. A serious-faced young man held up the card-reader for him to make his contactless payment. When Kevin came to the serving ledge, further on, one of the most amazing women he had ever seen in his life greeted him. She had an open, guileless face, dark-brown hair tied back in a ponytail. Kevin wondered if she undid the ponytail when she had sex.

'Kevin?' she said.

Kevin could hardly speak. Did she actually know him? She could have known him at uni and always had a kind of bittersweet quirky crush on him and this meeting could have reawakened feelings which... No. Actually he had given his name to the man at the till and it was written on his cup and also on his debit card.

'Here is your loyalty card. We'll stamp it every time you come in, and after nine stamps, you get a free latte!'

The card was square, light grey-blue in colour, made from a kind of pulpy, recycled cardboard, thick enough for its four corners to cut subtly into his palm, with a noughts-and-crosses-style nine-square reticulation. In the top left-hand square was his first stamp: the letter F, slightly overlapping the next square to the right.

'Thanks.'

Kevin moved away from the counter and found himself a table for one.

Then he took out his smartphone and from his @KevinDeTBone handle drafted a post: 'Loving the new Café Fidel on Piccadilly.' Sycophantically, he rephrased this: 'Loving the new @CafeFidel on Piccadilly' – to get the proprietor's attention.

He sent it.

Then he checked the time on his phone: 8.34am. More than enough time before work. He had chosen a seat he thought would allow him sight of the woman who had served him, but it was only after an elaborate series of pointless and unnoticed manoeuvres such as sipping his coffee, nibbling his Eccles cake and brushing the crumbs from his trousers, that he put this to the test by turning slightly in his seat and looking directly over in her direction. At that moment, he found that she was looking straight at him. Kevin convulsively swivelled back the way he had been facing, like someone on a fairground ride. He had a sunburst of flame on each cheek and spilt some coffee painfully on his wrist.

STAMP 2

Kevin had not intended to go back to Café Fidel. He had had a lot on his plate at work. Moreover, Café Fidel had 'liked' but not reposted his social media shout-out, for all the world as if it did not care to associate itself with Kevin's public reputation online.

But walking past at 8.20am, he found himself assessing his own reflection in Café Fidel's glass shopfront, and considered it just about satisfactory. Feeling in his pocket, he ran his fingertip against the edge of his Café Fidel loyalty card, which, being slightly too big for his wallet, poked out of it.

He went into Café Fidel. Ahead of him was the man with

the label. It was sort of halfway out of his neckline this time. Kevin could read the words 'hand wash'. He imagined poking it down with far more aggression than he had envisaged the last time; he pictured his fingernail jabbing down with obvious hostility into the man's neck as he restored the label, he felt the serration of his bitten nail slice into the light downy skin, and imagined the nail catching as it cut downwards, like a fish-hook.

8.22am.

This was taking slightly longer than he anticipated. There was nevertheless ample time for him to get his coffee and sugary snack and settle down at one of Café Fidel's unoccupied tables.

The customer ahead of him was just paying for his cappuccino when the man with Cthulhu tattooed on his neck appeared out of nowhere and very clearly touched Kevin's foot with the cold steel of his scooter wheel as he whooshed up to the counter.

'Mate! I need those eight cappos, yeah?'

There was now an inappropriate extra wait of four minutes while this man ordered his eight extra coffees, and his scooter came very close to Kevin as he whooshed out of Café Fidel. Kevin gave his card to the unsmiling young man, having made his own order, and then he took out his loyalty card. He saw that it no longer had its former pristine appearance but was creased along the top.

He handed it over to the man, who handed it to the woman with the ponytail alongside him.

Then Kevin noticed the tip jar on the counter in front of him, a feature which had survived the lockdown and the subsequent near-disappearance of cash. It was actually a large white cup whose handle had been broken off. A piece of card had been taped to its outside, reading: 'For the staff – thank you!!' The cup was full of dull bronze coins: twos and pennies. On a whim, Kevin took a pound coin from his pocket, a gratuity that constituted considerably more than 15 percent of the charge, and casually tossed it into the cup. It clinked against the rim, bounced out over the counter and rolled soundlessly off onto the floor while the stern assistant had his back to him. This barista turned and said briskly to the person on Kevin's right: 'Yes, please?'

Kevin had no choice but to move on without saying anything.

After a minute or so, the young woman said: 'Kevin?'

It was in a rather teasing, rather indulgent voice, Kevin thought. The kind of voice that you might use on your new boyfriend, who was nuzzlingly attempting to awaken you from your sensuous drowse early on a Sunday morning and engage in a new and vigorous bout of lovemaking, to which you would be resistant at first, but then moan and gasp with pleasure at—

'Kevin?'

With an utterly blank expression, she was holding the coffee marked with his name out to him with one hand. In the other was his loyalty card.

'Thank you,' he said submissively, and studied it as he walked, at least partly as a way of looking away from the woman's face.

STAMP 3

The next morning, Kevin came to Café Fidel with hardly any nerves at all, almost relieved that the woman did not seem to be on the till. Having had his card punched again, he took his coffee to his seat and opened his Instagram account. There was one photograph, unfiltered, unadorned – a selfie of Kevin with his elderly widowed father Ben, whom he had visited the previous weekend at the Kent cottage where he now lived alone. Kevin was wearing his strained smile and his father was leaning and peering into the lens the way he might into a well, or over the edge of a dangerous precipice.

Kevin opened his emails and found the one he had been expecting and dreading.

From: Ben@Benweb.com
To: KevinDeTrafford@dovercommercialholdings.co.uk

Dear Kevin,

Hello! Smashing to see you this weekend, although sad that Katherine is no longer with you. I liked her, and your mother certainly did.

I know you said that breaking up was a mutual decision and better for you both but frankly old boy that sounds like you were in receipt of the Big E! It sounds like you were standing there on the parade ground in the wind and rain while Katherine ceremoniously pinned the Order of the Boot on your manly chest. Forgive my old soldier's way of talking.

You mustn't worry about me. I know you do but don't. I'm perfectly all right. I've got my garden and my woodwork and I get into the town twice a week on the special bus.

Chin up!

Your

Dad xxxx

Kevin experienced a complicated clutch of emotions on reading this. He sipped his coffee. It had a takeaway lid on it. He guided it to his mouth by placing the tip of his tongue in the hole and bringing it up to his lips. Then he carefully prised the lid off, and placed it on the paper napkin he had brought over, so that the table surface would not become damp, and sipped again.

He looked over, and the young woman had appeared. But she had shaken her hair loose. She was on her phone. He looked around and saw that everyone in the whole of Café Fidel was on their phone, except for one customer, about whom he noticed something odd.

He was carrying an attaché case, walking around, peering vaguely about, perhaps searching for someone he had arranged to meet. It was the kind of thing you did in a coffee shop when you just wanted to use the lavatories without buying anything. But then this man went up to a table temporarily vacated by a smartly dressed young customer who had gone to get an extra sachet of sweetener, took the phone which she had left unattended on the table, and placed it smoothly into a sidepocket of his case. He went to someone else and did the same with the man's wallet, which was poking out of his jacket, which he had slung over a chair. Then, moving sinuously and unhurriedly, he walked over to a mother with a baby and took her purse from the bag she had distractedly placed on the ground. That too went into his case.

Kevin saw it all happening, with pin-sharp clarity. In a few moments more, he knew the man would be gone. In the days and weeks that followed, he would never be able to understand the burst of genius that now overcame him.

'Sir!' he called after the man. 'Wait!'

And he held out his own wallet to the man, who fatally paused near the door and turned towards him. For a fraction of a second, Kevin had created the impression that the man had dropped the wallet. He then walked towards the man, who remained still, apparently baffled, or perhaps believing that he might be able to pick up one extra fortuitously dropped wallet before making his escape.

But then Kevin boldly positioned himself between the man and the door. Close to, he could see a furtive, unshaven face, which did not meet his eye, but maintained a strange gaze down at the floor somewhere to Kevin's left.

'Stop,' Kevin said, putting his own wallet back into his pocket. 'Empty out that case. Call the police!' he then called out in a loud voice to the people behind the counter. 'This man has been stealing everyone's phones and wallets!'

The effect was electric. Everyone checked their pockets, and registered their missing property by standing up and then not moving. No one came to Kevin's aid. After all, the man could be armed, or rigged with a suicide-bomber's jacket. The male barista was calling someone on his mobile.

'Show me that case,' said Kevin, amazing himself with his courage.

The man now tried to push past Kevin who impeded him, grabbing hold of the case's handle. There was a bizarre scuffle. Still no one came to help. It was at this point that Kevin realised the thief might well hit him or stab him with some concealed blade or kung fu device. He could be seriously hurt. But no. It was just the scuffling over the case. Eventually the young woman came and stood in front of the door. The pulling and counter-pulling of the case continued. And finally, the man evidently made a decision to cut his losses, justifying Kevin's brilliant strategic decision to focus the confrontation on the case, rather than make it a direct physical combat. He let it go, wrenched open the door, hitting the woman painfully on the temple, and ran out into the street and down the pavement.

He was gone.

The music gulped out into silence. Kevin was left with the case in his hand. In that moment, he realised that he personally had taken responsibility for this whole situation. He was in fact anticipating or hoping for a little round of applause. Some gesture of heartfelt thanks. But no. No one spoke or moved, except the woman by the door, who asked him: 'Are you all right?' while holding her injured head.

'Thank you,' said Kevin, oddly, and then put the case down on a table and opened it. There was nothing inside, except a crumpled copy of the free daily newspaper handed out on the Underground. But feeling inside the bulging side pocket, he found dozens of wallets, purses and smartphones and proceeded to lay them out on the tabletop as energetically and methodically as if he had been preparing for this all morning.

'If people want to recover their property, they can do so now,' he announced, and this extraordinary display of public confidence used up the last scrap of his energy. Both of his legs now trembled uncontrollably and he had to sit down.

It was only now that Kevin realised he had actually been carrying his coffee in the other hand and that it had spilt all over his hip.

This was the moment at which the spell was broken. Everyone crowded round. They murmured: 'Thank you!' and 'Thanks mate!' Others offered to get him coffee and soon lattes and raisin swirls appeared on his table, next to the empty case. Kevin didn't realise it yet, but a number of people had taken pictures of him on their phones and were posting the most dramatic accounts of his heroism. It only occurred to him after some minutes to check the time. He was going to be late. He thought he should probably stay for the police. But had anyone actually called the police? Was there any point in doing that? He got ready to go. But then the woman who worked behind the till came up to him.

'Hi,' she said.

'Hi,' said Kevin.

'Look, we're really grateful for what you did, just now.'

'Not at all,' said Kevin.

'In theory, we're supposed to not, you know, "have a go" and we're supposed to dissuade people from "having a go". But never mind that. You had a go and you succeeded. Well done you. I actually really admire what you did. Oh, your card!'

She pointed to his loyalty card with its three stamps, which was lying on the tabletop beside him, mashed and sodden with spilt coffee.

'Let me replace that!'

The woman rushed away and soon came back with a brand new card, with four crisp, sharp corners and three 'F' stamps in the boxes where the other ones had been. Kevin took it from her and put it carefully in his wallet.

'I'm Helen by the way,' she said.

'I'm Kevin,' replied Kevin.

'Yes I know,' she said brightly. 'It's always on your latte. And you're getting to be a regular.'

'Oh yes! Of course!'

There was a pause, made more uncomfortable by the fact that people were crowding around them, people who felt that they had not quite yet discharged their responsibility to thank

Kevin, and people who were fascinated by this conversation between the coffee-related hero and a coffee-shop official. They eavesdropped quite openly, and felt they were entitled to participate in the conversation in this way. It was like the court of a Bourbon king.

'Have you worked here long?' asked Kevin.

'Oh about four months,' said Helen.

'What did you do before that?' he asked.

'Graduated drama school. What about you – where do you work?'

'Oh, I work at a place called Dover Commercial Holdings in Dover Street, just round the corner. We advise on investments. It's pretty dull really!'

He shrugged and smiled self-deprecatingly. The conversation appeared to be at an end.

Kevin returned to the seat he was occupying at the back of the café. He was just about to place his renewed loyalty card back into his wallet when he turned it over and saw there was writing on the back:

Helen 07740 255595

STAMP 4

Kevin thought hard before coming back to Café Fidel.

It wasn't simply that he didn't know how or if to act on what he had seen written on the back of his loyalty card. He didn't know what to do at all. He didn't know how to prioritise his personal life and his business commitments. He didn't know if he should come into the café in the morning, the way he had been doing, or make a breezy appearance at lunchtime, or arrive just before it closed at eight o'clock on the 'what time do you get off?' basis he had seen in films.

He really didn't know what his next move was.

Helen. 07740 255595.

Should he call her? Should he text her?

As demurely self-conscious as a bride processing down the aisle with her father on her arm, Kevin now entered Café Fidel for the fourth time. It was lunchtime. He casually looked at a copy of a report he had written for the human resources department, a considerable internal success. It had resulted in staffing rationalisations for which he had been personally thanked by the Chief Operating Officer.

Pretending to be entirely absorbed, Kevin didn't look up as he gave his order for a latte, and an Emmental and prosciutto bap. He took his coffee and his card with its fourth stamp, still pretending to be fascinated by what he was reading. It was the man who served him. Not Helen. Kevin sat down.

He couldn't call her, certainly not here. That would be ridiculous. Surely it would be more casual to begin a conversation in the café itself?

Or should he maybe reach our on her socials?

That was a point. He didn't have her last name. Yet it occurred to Kevin that by finding the Café Fidel timeline, he should be able to find her online footprint: the café itself would have mentioned her as its own prominent employee.

Wait.

What was this?

A post had come up. Kevin clicked on it, and at first he registered a photograph of someone he thought that he recognised: a short man with a double chin sitting in the café itself, surrounded by people, a case on the table in front of him. The picture was a little unclear – perhaps taken from a distance, with a zoom. Kevin felt that stinging metallic lurch in his bloodstream on realising that this was a picture of him. It said: *This guy is my hero. He totally challenged a thief in here. Thank you sir!*

Kevin had to re-read this repeatedly just to acclimatise himself to it and bring his heart rate down. 'My' hero. Not our hero. My hero. Who has written this? Could it have been Helen? He looked again at the photograph and noticed a female profile to the left of the frame. It was Helen, smiling at him. His intense stab of pleasure at seeing this for a moment cancelled his realisation that the author was therefore not in fact Helen. It was the person taking the picture. Presumably the young man. But maybe not. He could have shared the picture with Helen and she could have posted it. He really was very short with a double chin. She was chatting to him out of pure pity. It was a pity chat. The sort you might have with an elderly relative at the beginning of a family party. But even if it was a pity chat, it could easily morph into pity sex. Or rather respect sex. It could well be an example of that very well-known thing whereby extremely attractive people have respect sex with people that they respect. It was a version of the respect sex that he had with himself many times, especially recently, after drinking half a bottle of red wine: sessions of solo respect sex which concluded with solemn tears shed in earnest tribute to the courage with which he withstood the awful pain of his loneliness.

Kevin could feel himself welling up.

The double-chinned image of himself on the phone blurred and swam as his eyes pricked, and the picture became momentarily more flattering.

He would have to go back to work soon, and that caused a new wave of dread and misery.

Why was work so horrible? Why did it always make him feel that he was in trouble, or as if he was attempting to work off through good behaviour some kind of lenient punishment for trouble he had got himself into – the way he had felt in school? And yet the actual work he did in school never made him feel like this.

He reached into his jacket pocket and took out the little bottle. Xanax – generic name, Alprazolam; 0.5mg, three times a day. He had already his morning one. He knew that it wasn't cool to do another one so soon.

He took out the loyalty card. Four stamps. Five to go. What would happen when he reached the ninth and final stamp? Well, he knew. He would get a free latte. And a new loyalty card. But would he keep coming here? Would he get to know Helen any better? Would he ever call her on that number? Would that be a catastrophic misjudgement? Was it all just a misunderstanding?

He checked his phone again. He was always checking his phone. He checked it hundreds of times a day, the way everyone did in real life and no one did on TV and in films. The @CafeFidel account had posted another photograph of him, looking thoughtful and upset. The accompanying text read: 'Why not download our ordering app?' though this was not directed at him in particular, but generally addressed. The picture had apparently been taken about twenty seconds previously. Kevin looked up and saw nothing and no one in front of him. He could see the grumpy young man at the counter, but not Helen. He was reading.

That was it. She was flirting with him. This whole thing was a massive meet-cute. It was time to take the plunge. Kevin texted Helen: *Hi. Very gratified to appear in your timeline! I was hoping to see you today - or maybe foil a kidnapping or jewel robbery here!*

There was a tiny delay and then the reply came: *Just trying to get your attention!*

And that was it. Kevin waited for any possible follow-up and once he was sure he wasn't going to tread on some delicately romantic second text, he typed out: *Where are you actually?*

Minute after minute went past. Helen didn't reply. Kevin had to go back to work.

STAMP 5

The next morning, Kevin got into line for a breakfast brioche and double cappuccino and once again found himself behind the man with the label sticking up out of his T-shirt. But this time the man was with a woman, who affectionately reached around and put his label back down under the material, and they exchanged a little hug.

Kevin was desolate. He was without hugs. He had never felt so utterly hugless. The other night, in his flat, he had experimentally tried to hug himself, a kind of platonic self-pleasuring which involved crossing his arms around his ribcage and placing his palms around his back at waist-level. It felt like he was preparing for a straitjacket.

He was almost in a position to order his coffee, pay for his chocolate brioche and receive the fifth stamp on his loyalty card, which he would then return to his wallet, when the man with the Cthulhu tattoo suddenly appeared in front of him, this time with another, slightly larger image of Cthulhu on the other side of his neck.

He told the person in front of the man with the label back inside his T-shirt: 'Mate! Sorry I'm late again. Need those nine coffees, yeah? And you know what? I'm treating myself. I'm getting a fuck-off-sized poppyseed cookie with the frosting. You know why? Because I'm only getting fucking married that's all!'

He beamed delightedly at the people in the line which he was holding up.

'I'm getting *married*,' he said again. 'I asked her last night and she said yes. Christ. What a performance. Married.' The man he was speaking to appeared to make some gesture of reservation or demurral.

'Yes well, there's that,' said the Cthulhu man, irritably. 'I'll have to get the divorce through but otherwise there's no bother, is there?'

Kevin was soon back in his seat, and was about to indulge in another reverie of self-pity when Helen came and pertly sat down opposite him.

'Hello,' she said. 'You were going to call me. Why haven't you called me?'

'Oh. Oh!' he said, trying not to soil himself in shock and over-excitement. 'I just, I don't…I don't know. Of course I was going to. Hello, by the way.'

'Playing it cool, of course. Relishing the ball being in your court. Well, *players* like you…' (She whimsically exaggerated an American accent) '…can miscalculate that sort of thing, you know. You can leave it too long. We can lose interest.'

'Oh, I'm…not at all…'

'Oh please,' said Helen. 'I'm just messing. We haven't found that man yet, by the way. For some reason the CCTV wasn't working. How are you?'

'Oh, you know, I'm fine,' said Kevin, and to stop the conversation faltering, asked: 'What did you say you did before working here?'

'I did drama school.'

'And have you worked since then?'

'Yes, I did a one-woman version of Sylvia Plath's *The Bell Jar* at the Edinburgh Fringe and I've actually been in a TV adaptation of *Tess of the d'Urbervilles*.'

'Really?'

'Yes. I had a very small part, I play Izzy Huett, one of the, you know, bucolic maidens that Tess knows. It was on last night, actually, I don't know if you saw it?''

'No. I'm sorry.'

'So anyway,' said Helen, forcefully. 'I wondered if I could say thank you, by inviting you to, ah, hang out with Stu and me. Sort of backstage.'

'Backstage?'

'Yes. We tend to call the counter the stage, and out here, front of house. Stu and I thought you might like to come and hang out with us there.'

'When?'

'Well, sort of, now.'

Kevin checked the time on his phone. He still had around twenty or so minutes before he needed to be in the office.

'Well – OK.'

Awkwardly, they both stood up, and with a little beckoning gesture Helen motioned him to follow her as she walked up to the service counter and round to the side. It was with a sense of transgression that Kevin entered that part of the café where he, as a customer, was not allowed to go. The man serving appeared to catch Helen's eye with an unreadable expression of complicity. Kevin continued to follow her, and looked down to see a silvery glint from the floor, from something half-concealed beneath a heavy cabinet set into the wall which contained bags of coffee from all over the world.

It was the pound coin he had attempted to throw into the tip jar.

Helen opened a door next to this cabinet, which he had never noticed before, and they walked together through a disshevelled office whose private squalor and gloominess made a sudden almost upsetting contrast with the immaculate, carefully lit public space of Café Fidel. It was lit only by the daylight coming into the window on the far wall. There was a swing bin in the corner, beside which, on the floor, squatted brown used teabags like the turds of a distressed animal which had accidentally got into the room and couldn't find its way out.

'Come through,' smiled Helen, and she took him through another corridor and up to a steel exit door which was bisected by the kind of bar which would usually trigger an alarm if it was pushed down. Helen pushed it down and the door judderingly swung open to reveal a small enclosed courtyard bounded on all four sides by whitewashed brick walls, in which was a closed door, through which he presumed they would take the bins, now clustered in one corner, out to the street from which he could hear traffic.

And leaning up against one of these walls was the other man, the one he so often saw in Helen's company. He was smoking a spliff with the length and girth of a cigar. Helen removed it from his lips and put it in her own. The man simply picked up the can of strong lager which he had down by his feet. It was half past eight in the morning.

'Here he is,' he said, with a derisive smile, lifting his can in a satirical 'cheers' motion. Instantly, Kevin felt the urge to apologise, as if he had been patronising in simply being here.

Helen offered the spliff to Kevin, pincered between finger and thumb.

'You want some? A taste?'

Kevin gave his standard shy-refusal smile and the little shake of the head looking down – to indicate a reluctance both to participate and to do anything which could be construed as disapproval.

'Fucking live a little,' said the man. 'Have some.'

'No. Really.'

'It's good enough for Helen and me,' Stu continued, grumpily.

'Stu, now come on,' said Helen severely, interrupting. 'You've had enough. I want you to get back to the kitchen, get some Tic Tacs down you and then get back to work. And apologise. Apologise to Kevin.'

'Sorry, mate,' said Stu as he left. 'Just a joke. I was just trying to, you know, lighten the mood.'

'I'm sorry about that,' said Helen with a grimace. 'Stu's not really like that. It's not him. Once you get to know him, he's really sweet.'

Kevin had never been more sure of anything in his life than his sudden, profound conviction that Stu did not get sweeter the more you knew him. Helen coolly leant back on the wall in the same attitude as Stu. She took a brief puff of the spliff and then waved it whimsically, almost absentmindedly around, apparently thinking about something else, as if trying to perfume the air between them, in lieu of Kevin's actually partaking.

'I meant what I said about admiring what you did, you know.'

'Oh, OK, yes, thanks.'

'Not everyone could have done that. Stu certainly couldn't have done. Afterwards, he told me that he didn't know what was going on. But he knew. He knew and just wouldn't get involved. You got involved. You did the business.'

She smoked again. They listened to the birdsong, incongruously loud above the bee-like traffic noise.

'Working in the coffee shop isn't all that bad,' she then ventured. 'I was actually lucky to get the job. Being a barista is quite highly prized.' The sun came out, and Helen stretched against the brickwork, languorously, or as if theatrically acknowledging acclaim for this professional success.

'Mmm,' he said, noncommittally.

'Christ. Fuck.'

Helen grabbed Kevin roughly by the shoulder, while keeping her joint clutched in the other hand, and shoved him round into a space where the non-join of two different heights of brick wall created a kind of alcove, in which they were invisible from the back door. And it was by this now open door that a man in his thirties was now standing, wearing a suit and sunglasses. Kevin had got the briefest glimpse of him while he was being shoved, but now the man was out of sight – as he and Helen presumably were to him.

Helen held Kevin in a tight, intimate embrace; her hand was round in the small of her back. Then she brought her other hand up so that she could make a 'shhh' gesture with her finger on her lips and they were so close that this finger was almost on Kevin's lips as well. She stared with desperate seriousness directly into Kevin's eyes, and mouthed: 'It's the manager. I'm not supposed to be out here, smoking weed.'

'Tanya,' said the man calmly. And then again: 'Tanya.' The

voice was quieter and more muted this second time, and Kevin guessed that he had ducked back outside. Then silence.

And Helen was holding him as tight as ever. Their faces were very close. After a few moments of silence, the evident danger of their being discovered receded, and consequently the danger of Kevin getting a prominent erection became a serious worry. It was to forestall this that he took it upon himself to break free of their clinch without Helen signalling that it was all right. After all, it wasn't he, Kevin, the customer, who was going to get into trouble. He should assert himself.

'Who's Tanya?'

'Oh. Yes, that's me. I didn't want to put my real name on my CV. Long story. Long story. My last employer was a bit of a dick; he made a pass at me and turned ugly when I didn't respond. I didn't want him giving me a bad reference for this.'

'The *Tess* guy?'

'Eh?'

'The guy in charge of the *Tess* shoot. When you acted in *Tess of the d'Urbervilles?*'

'Oh. That. No. Not that. Nothing to do with that.'

Helen unwound enough to take another drag. She smiled.

'Anyway, I'm sorry about that. But you handled yourself pretty well, I think. Pretty cool. What's the most illegal thing you've ever done?'

'When I was ten I recorded a TV show on video without a licence, in flagrant contravention of the Wireless Telegraphy Act, 1949.'

It was a line he'd used before. Helen laughed as she shepherded him back round into the main section of the café, and for the remaining few minutes he could be there, they exchanged flirtatious little smiles.

STAMP 6

When Kevin came to the café the next day – which was a Saturday – Helen wasn't there. He bought a coffee, called her while he was drinking it, but went straight through to a generic voicemail, so he hung up.

STAMP 7

Kevin knew he shouldn't, but he returned on Sunday as well, to buy yet another coffee from the deadpan Stu, who gave no indication of ever having met him. Helen wasn't there. He didn't call her.

STAMP 8

Kevin was quite well aware that his behaviour was becoming obsessive and odd. He understood that Helen had not been at the café over the past two days because it was the weekend. She was doing something else. Naturally. And that was none of his business. He should himself have been doing something else with his weekend, instead of obsessing about her. But when he returned to Café Fidel on Monday, he timed it for 7.45pm, not very long before it closed at eight. He hardly dared admit to himself that he hoped to invite Helen out somewhere afterwards.

There weren't many other people there. Helen was the only person serving and greeted him roguishly: 'Hello darling!'

Poor Kevin blushed to the roots of his hair and trembled as he received the eighth stamp on his now dog-eared card.

Ten minutes after he was seated – and no longer attempting to play anything cool, Kevin faced her and took every opportunity to catch her eye and smile – Helen sauntered over and sat down.

'Hello you,' she said and Kevin felt his heart literally turn over.

'Hello.'

'I was thinking, Kevin. Do you have a girlfriend? Or boyfriend?'

'No. We broke up. Her name was Katherine,' he added, redundantly.

'I bet she dumped you and broke your heart,' said Helen, callously.

Kevin was about to deny it, indignantly, but then simply gave a defeated nod.

'I know what it's like to have a broken heart, you know,' Helen said, seriously. 'My heart's been broken so long I can't remember when it was whole.'

The two sat in silence for a while, before Kevin said: 'What are you doing after this? Do you fancy coming with me to the pub?'

'Oh Kevin. That's so sweet. I'd have loved to normally. But I'm supposed to be meeting someone. Look – are you coming in tomorrow?'

'Yes, of course.'

'You loyal darling. Come in at 1pm and I'll have something for you.'

STAMP 9

Kevin had dressed up a little more for this rendezvous. Or rather: he dressed down. That uncool tie that he had to wear in the office, and which he usually kept on, was now removed and stuffed in the jacket pocket of what he hoped was his trendiest-looking suit.

When he came in, he had to wait a long time. The lunchtime

crush was immense. But Helen and he saw each other straight away and they even exchanged little waves, she with her elbow down at her waist, and a grin: a simperingly girlish effect that didn't entirely suit her.

He had a BLT and an orange juice from the fridge cabinet; Helen ceremoniously gave his card its final stamp and said in a whisper: 'You'll get your reward in a minute.'

Kevin almost fainted with happiness.

He sat in his usual seat, impatiently expecting to be called behind the counter and into their special secret space. And so it proved.

Helen checked the time on her phone, looked up and beckoned Kevin forward with a curling forefinger. He jumped up and came round: Helen held up the counter flap while someone else – another woman, not the sullen Stu – dealt with the customers.

In a moment, they found themselves once again in that brick-walled outside space, although Kevin noticed that the back door was slightly open. With a flourish, Helen took out a pre-rolled spliff, lit it and handed it to Kevin, who now recklessly took a drag.

'Well, Kevin, I'm seeing a new side of you.'

After a few minutes in which the spliff was wordlessly passed back and forth, Kevin said: 'Helen, do you want to go on holiday with me?'

Helen laughed, but uneasily, and checked her phone again. 'Holiday, Kevin? Where?'

'I don't know; Greece. Italy. Croatia.'

'Sharing a room?'

'Maybe, yeah,' said Kevin, whose sense of moody sensual defiance was now approaching that of a young Marlon Brando.

'Sharing a bed?'

Kevin pressed his lips together and said: 'Yeah. Yes. Totally. I'd like that. Would you?'

Suddenly, Helen's phone cheeped. She had a text. She looked at her phone intently and then looked up, over his shoulder. Kevin sensed that she was not trying to decide whether or not to sleep with him on holiday.

'Tanya,' said a voice behind him. He froze. The manager. Was Helen going to get into trouble? Why was she making no attempt to hide?

Kevin turned around and looked into a very familiar face. The speaker was the man with the attaché case whom he'd caught stealing all the wallets. As before, the side pocket was bulging with booty.

'Hello mate,' he said with a dangerous, quiet smile. 'Good to see you again. How are you?' He appeared to require an answer.

'OK,' said Kevin numbly.

'You made quite an impression on my girlfriend here, you know. Quite an impression. She rather took to you, I think.'

Kevin nervously began to say: 'I didn't know that…'

But the man held up a hand: 'Please don't worry. Tanya explained to me that it amused her to befriend you, despite the problems you caused. She promised me that was all it was. Looking at you, I can believe it. But I think she did sort of like you, in a way.' He caught the eye of Helen, or rather Tanya, before looking back at Kevin. 'I like you too. You've got balls.'

Kevin's mouth opened and closed soundlessly.

'Mind you,' the man added, playfully wagging a finger rather too close to Kevin's face. 'That day when I popped round back here unannounced. Do you remember? That day you and Tanya hid from me.' He brought his face menacingly close to Kevin's. 'You naughty children.'

After a beat, he stepped back and went on: 'Tanya told me afterwards it was so you wouldn't see my face, and you'd think it was the manager. That was really quick thinking on her part. But I wonder if she wasn't partly just a little bit worried about how I would react to seeing you together.'

Again, he looked at Tanya, who looked away, then back to Kevin, who didn't know where to look.

'Well, Tanya had to get you out here now, so you wouldn't do your have-a-go hero routine again while I collected up everyone's gear.'

Now Tanya stepped forward and said sadly: 'I had to delete that CCTV.'

Perhaps she had more to say to Kevin, but her boyfriend interrupted: 'Well, now we've got to go. We've got a ferry to catch.'

Holding hands, the pair of them ducked through the door, beyond which Kevin could see a parked motorbike. Tanya gave him an infinitesimally brief little goodbye smile. And then the man suddenly reappeared, and pressed something uncomfortably hot into Kevin's hand.

'I'm so sorry Kevin! I totally forgot. Here it is! You deserve it! No charge!'

He left again, and as the bike roared away, Kevin looked down at his cooling latte in the takeaway cup, the loyalty card tucked into its sleeve.

ACKNOWLEDGEMENTS

Reunion, Neighbours of Zero and *Senior Moment* were first broadcast on BBC Radio 4. *The Kiss, My Pleasure* and *All This Aggravation* were originally published in *Confingo Magazine*. *Holiness* appeared first in *Esquire*.

I have to begin by acknowledging the late David Miller, who was my agent and friend for over twenty years: a brilliant writer, reader, Conrad scholar and connoisseur of the short story. David was taken from us much too soon. Now my agent is the abundantly clever and kind Sam Copeland at Rogers, Coleridge and White.

Jon Naismith was the original BBC Radio producer and script editor on my work; Duncan Minshull at BBC Radio has been hugely important to my writing, and I should also thank Di Speirs and Justine Willett for their encouragement, and of course Dan Hiscocks and Simon Edge at Lightning Books.

Nicholas Royle has published my work at *Confingo*, and he is an inspirational evangelist for the short story form. Alex Bilmes at *Esquire* is a brilliant editor and stylish man about town: the phrase 'good company' doesn't cover it. Tom Hollander, Daniel Mays and Michael Maloney superbly read my stories aloud on Radio 4.

I want to thank Sarah Bradshaw and Roy Mehta — and lastly and most importantly my wife, Caroline Hill and my son, Dominic. I love and owe them more than I can say.

If you have enjoyed *The Body in the Mobile Library & Other Stories*, do please help us spread the word – by putting a review online; by posting something on social media; or in the old-fashioned way by simply telling your friends or family about it.

Book publishing is a very competitive business these days, in a saturated market, and small independent publishers such as ourselves are often crowded out by the big houses. Support from readers like you can make all the difference to a book's success.

Many thanks.

Dan Hiscocks
Publisher
Lightning Books